LINES ON THE PALM

LINES ON THE PALM

DIANA NURI

Diana Nuri

Contents

Prologue — vii

1
LINES ON THE PALM

2
HATE

3
WHOSE FAULT IS IT?

4
THE CHOICE

5
PLAYING PRETEND

6

THE WORLD OF SNAKES

7
THINKING OUT LOUD

Prologue

Prologue

Different stories about different lives, united by one thing—strength. The only difference is that some use it for good, while some use it for ill.

In my work, I often meet older women who have faced severe injustices in their childhood. At the beginning of their journey, they are united and haunted by the same question—what did I do to deserve this? Some accept their new reality and rise to the surface, realizing that there is no answer to this question, but others cannot. It is a great pity, for I always say, no matter what happens in our lives, we must live! We must keep fighting. No matter what and despite everything! We must overcome these difficulties and move on, despite, at times, unbearable hardships. Believe me, we have the strength to persevere, because, as the Bible says, God "will not let you be tried beyond what you are able to bear." I agree that life can be cruel, unfair, and knock us down so hard that we cannot stand back up. And yet we do. We find the fuel in our empty tank, and we stand back up, because the fire of our indomitable spirit burns within us. It is genuinely invincible. I have great respect for and pride in women. I truly believe that no one in the world is stronger than us. The strength, love, care, bravery, daring, patience, and *courage in our cannot only warm those in need, but literally bring the whole World into a brighter future.*

From the bottom of my heart, I wish you the resilience to endure all hardships, for every trial comes to an end one day. I believe that each of you can create your own happiness, build your own world, and fulfil your dreams. God bless you.

With love,

Diana Nuri

I

Lines on the palm

Lines on the palm
A Novel

Jess sat in a rocking chair by the slightly open window, studying the lines on her palms. How often had she covered her face with these palms from blows, tears, and grief over the years? How many times had she clenched them into fists, hating the world, her life, all of creation and God? Many years had passed, yet she remembered those events in miniscule detail. Unexpectedly, she burst into tears.

Jess was born sometime between April 8 and 13. No one knows the exact date, because her mother was high when she gave birth to Jess at home and presented to the hospital much later. Incredibly, the girl was born healthy, despite her parents' immoral lifestyle. She was a calm, fuss-free child. Even if she had caused any trouble, however, no one would have dealt with it. Perhaps the girl's trouble-free nature stemmed from learned hopelessness.

Her mother felt completely indifferent toward her, while her father expressed something akin to love. He would often pick her up and throw her high in the air, laughing loudly. She remembered his bright blue eyes and snow-white teeth.

Jess was first taken to a children's home at around 2 years of age. Her mother fell asleep with a cigarette in hand after going on yet another bender, and started a fire, nearly killing herself and her daughter. She somehow managed to get Jess back despite what had happened. As it later turned out, her father insisted on this, threatening to leave the family otherwise. Jess's mother had no choice but to pull herself together and quit her addictions for a while. The family lived without any tragedies for the next three years. What remained unchanged were the scandals, fights, and the terrible lack of money. From that time in her life, Jess would remember the dilapidated grey trailer, the fat cockroaches in the kitchen and the nasty smell of her mother's concoctions.

By the age of five, Jess had already seen the dark side of life, experiencing hunger, hopelessness, helplessness, and despair. She now had two younger sisters. They were sweet and gentle girls with wheat-blonde curls. Jess loved them with all her heart and tried to take care of them as best as she could. Later, as an adult, she would often remember them and wonder why such wonderful kids were born yet did not receive the necessary love, care, and attention. Why were they cursed with such a life?

The most revolting memory from childhood was one of her father's friends looking at her with glassy eyes, gripping her arm tightly and running his finger over her lips, saying what a beautiful girl she was. As an adult, Jess would freeze in fear whenever someone mentioned her beauty.

Jess's father died when she was six years old. She remembered the pool of blood in the living room and the knife sticking out of his stomach. She was finally taken to a children's home, together with her younger sisters.

Things went well at the start. For the first time in their lives, the girls were cared for and someone might have even loved them. They had their own beds, clean sheets, clothes, and food. It all smelled so wonderful! Jess couldn't get enough of the scent of freshly pressed bed linen. She finally felt safe and calm within the walls of the children's home. Her only fear was that she would be returned to her mother, and this fear persisted for a long time. Jess would freeze every time she heard her last name, listening intently to every word.

One cold and cloudy day, Jess was summoned to the director's office for no apparent reason. When Jess entered the office and saw a strange woman, the girl immediately tensed up. She paused at the door, hesitant to approach the table.

"Come and sit down, Jessica," Mrs. Fort said gently, pointing to a chair beside the stranger.

The girl came over quietly and perched on the edge of the chair.

"I want to introduce you to someone. This is Miss Meadow."

"Hello," Jess said without lifting her eyes.

"Miss Meadow has visited us several times, and she really likes you. She's willing to take you home with her."

Jess was silent.

"Why aren't you saying anything, Jess?" Miss Meadow asked. "Aren't you glad?"

The woman's voice was gentle, and Jess finally glanced up at her. Miss Meadow was an attractive woman in her forties. She wore no make-up, so it seemed like she had no eyelashes at all. Her black eyebrows stood out against hair tinged with silver, which was pulled neatly back in a bun.

"I'm glad," the girl replied.

"Me too. I'll visit you while the paperwork is being done, so that we can become friends. It'll make our lives easier afterwards."

"Will you take Esme and Bella too?"

"Shh, that's enough, go back to your room!" Mrs. Fort became abruptly angry.

Jess grew more and more terrified on her walk back. She didn't want to live with a woman she didn't know. She also guessed that she would have to say goodbye to her sisters, perhaps forever.

"Well?" Melissa, whose bed stood beside Jess's, asked enthusiastically.

"I think I'm getting adopted."

"Congratulations! What's wrong? Why aren't you happy?"

"I'll be separated from Esme and Bella."

"Maybe they'll get adopted too!"

Jess didn't answer, burying her face in the pillow.

True to her word, Miss Meadow visited the home every day. Her name turned out to be Victoria. A beautiful, royal name. She seemed to be a good woman overall. She was calm, sweet, and talked about her life and the reasons why she decided to adopt.

Victoria Meadow came from a conservative family. Her father died early, and her mother did not remarry but raised her alone. When she was 20 years old, Victoria met a young man and fell madly in love with him, and he with her. It was first love, pure and naive. Victoria dreamed of the day she would marry him and give him children with hazel eyes like his own, but her mother had other plans. When she learned that her daughter was in a relationship and had even been intimate with a man from another denomination, she threw all her effort into destroying the union. Oh, if only this horror had remained behind closed doors! Victoria had to endure a lot. Harsh beatings, as well as vile and disgusting insults. She endured not only her relatives, but all her neighbours discovering what a "trollop" she was. Nevertheless, this was not what destroyed the Victoria's soul forever, but what her mother did afterwards. After finding out the young man's address, her mother marched over there and made such a scene that her daughter could no longer show her face on the street. The whole neighbourhood learned of the scandal. The intimidating woman had such an effect on the handsome young man's parents that they forbade him from coming close to Victoria, afraid of her, the courts, police, and everything else she threatened them with. Victoria was taken to a distant village to stay with her grandmother, where she had to pray to God for days on end and beg forgiveness for her immoral behaviour. Of course, she did not share these details with the child, but the pain of this experience had left its mark on her. She often wondered how her life would have turned out if her mother had been different. Was it her mother's fault that Victoria's life was far from happy, and that at the age of 44, she lacked what she had dreamed of since childhood? An apartment instead of a house, emptiness instead of love, and a hated job at the tax department instead of an exciting business of her own. She was lonely and deeply unhappy, and she felt sorry for herself. A pity that she had been laid low by either life itself, or her stupid mother.

When the big day came, Jess hugged her sisters for the last time. She had tried to prepare them for the upcoming separation, but she did not expect it to be so painful. The little girls cried and clutched at her clothes as if their lives depended on it. The carers had to pry the children away from each other. Jess stared at the windows of the home for a long time before following Victoria Meadow. When she reached the tram stop, the child suddenly asked, "Please, can't you take my sisters too? They won't get in the way, and we won't be any trouble."

"No. I haven't told anyone about one child, let alone three! Besides, as far as I know, they've also found a new family."

Jess's heart shattered into pieces. Was this really the last time she would see her siblings?

"Have you ever been on a tram?" Miss Meadow asked, trying to distract the girl.

"No."

"Fun, isn't it?"

"Yeah."

"You should forget everything that happened to you before and start life afresh. Deal?"

Jess nodded without looking at her.

Jess's new abode was on the other side of the city from the children's home. It was an unusual suburb, and Jess had never seen one like it before. Clean streets, beautiful and well-kept courtyards with shrubs and flowers, and equally charming 5-storey houses. Miss Meadow's apartment was on the fourth floor. Jess noticed that the woman clearly loved order when she stepped inside. The interior was quite frugal, with a simple sofa and TV in the living room and two beds at either end of the bedroom. A plinth with enormous religious icons stood in each room, which made Jess feel strangely uneasy. Thus began a new chapter in the little girl's life. A life devoid of joy. But she would discover this later.

Jess went to school and got used to new routines and rules, of which there were a great many at Mrs. Meadow's house. Absolutely everything was forbidden. She could not watch TV, she could not be idle, she could not sing or listen to music. Jess was expected to start on her homework after school and remain sitting at her desk when her new mother came home. Only after Miss Meadow had checked her homework and was satisfied with how much she had done was Jess allowed to get up and eat dinner. She was expected to pray every night before bed.

Jess would often hear Miss Meadow crying at night. She did not dare to ask why, or rather, she was afraid, so she lay in bed as quiet as a mouse. For some reason, the woman scared the girl more and more with every passing day. Jess could not understand why Mrs. Meadow had adopted her, because their relationship was not at all like that of a mother and daughter. There was no tenderness, nor the slightest display of love or care that she noticed in others.

As Jess neared 12 years of age and began to display signs of femininity and individuality, Miss Meadow's attitude towards her changed rapidly. The woman she now called Mom turned into an exact copy of her own mother. Miss Meadow was irritated by everything Jess said and did. This was when the beatings began. While the girl no longer paid attention to the insults, rules and prohibitions, the physical violence elicited terrible emotional anguish. Coming to school with a scratched face and dishevelled hair became the norm. How strange that not a single person in the school noticed or helped her.

Jess was punished for anything at all, and often for no reason at all. Things were especially horrible whenever her mother had a bad day at work. Victoria took out her unexpressed frustration with work on the girl. It was not until many years later that Jess understood the real reason for this behaviour. There was nothing wrong with Jess herself, she just wasn't *her* Jess. She was some strange girl whose features did not remind Victoria of the man she had once loved. The adult Jess realized that Miss Meadow had adopted her to fix her unhappy life, unaware that this was not how it worked. Only *you* can make yourself happy. Not a child, not a kitten, only you. Jess was like a toy, bought because Victoria thought it would make her happy. When Victoria realized that the child did not bring her joy, she began to hate her fiercely. How was that Jess's fault?

Jess was about 13 years old when her mother first called her a prostitute. The word was so vile that she wanted to take a shower afterwards. Jess didn't know why her mother would say that because she was completely clean. At night, choking back tears, the girl prayed for death. Jess imagined Miss Meadow crying at her funeral and sincerely wishing she had valued her daughter more when she was still alive.

To Jess's disappointment, death did not hear her, and things continued as before.

One dreary Saturday morning, her mother woke her up very early. Victoria was in unusually high spirits.

"You're going to help me clean the house and cook dinner tonight. And you'll be going Grandma's for the night," Mom said, dragging the girl out of bed.

"Yes, Mom," Jess said dutifully.

"You'll be back tomorrow evening. I'm expecting someone."

This someone arrived earlier than expected and Jess saw that it was a man. She was surprised since her mother had never brought men home before.

"Get out of here," Mom hissed, shoving the girl's sandals into her hands. "And not a word of this to Grandma!"

After being roughly pushed out the door, Jess sat down on the cold steps, and buried her face in her hands. She got up only when she heard footsteps coming down from above. She descended the stairs, opened the door, and was momentarily blinded by the sunlight. Spring! A time of joy, but sadly, not for everyone.

Jess wandered the streets, staring at the windows of other houses. She imagined the life taking place inside those walls: music drifting from one apartment, and the sound of laughter from another. Surely, a table was being set right now, people sitting down, thanking one another for the meal, and only she had nowhere to go. She did not belong anywhere. Her own mother had not loved her and neither did her foster mother. Not a single person in the whole world was willing to show her affection and warm her frozen heart. How much had her heart suffered already?!

"On the other hand," Jess muttered, "you shouldn't feel sorry for yourself. It's not that bad, you have food and a roof over your head." 'Ha!' Laughed her inner voice. 'What about love? Everyone wants to love and to be loved and needed. Such is our nature and love are important to us. Perhaps it is one of the conditions for human survival?'

Jess had not noticed that she had automatically walked to her grandmother's house. She sat down on the swing and gazed up at the bright blue sky. What a big and vast world this was! So many people and destinies. Who created it all? What if we are all ants on someone's farm? Someone who watches each of us, moving us hither and thither. It's just a game to him, and he doesn't even know that we are suffering. Who can know?

Grandma leaned out of the window and screeched across the whole yard, "Why are you sitting there, lazybones? Come inside."

Jess looked at the wrinkled face, got up from the swing, and reluctantly wandered inside. As she climbed the stairs, her only thought was that today, at least, she would get enough to eat, enough sleep and would not be beaten. Yes, the chores at her grandmother's house could be hard, but unlike her daughter, the old woman did not starve the girl and let Jess to eat as much as she wanted.

"What are you doing here?" Grandma asked rudely.

"Mom has friends over and I'm in the way."

"Friends over! Shameless woman! She should be taking care of her child. She doesn't help, she doesn't call for years, yet she sends her fosterling over! Ungrateful trash! I raised her, and for what? What are you staring at? Go and eat. I'll finish watching the show and then I'll find you something to do."

Grandma, of course, gave Jess chores to do since she couldn't sit around doing nothing. But after Jess finished them, she could finally sit and watch TV like any normal person. Grandma did not scold her for this.

Jess did not want to return to her mother the next day, and she waited anxiously for the phone to ring. To her delight, it only rang late in the evening.

From that day forth, Jess stayed with her grandmother quite often, because Victoria's man stuck around. His name was Nick, and he seemed like a decent person, apart from being dreadfully boring. But Jess was grateful to him, because for the first time in her life, her mother shifted her attention to someone else, and beat the girl a little less. A year passed this way. Jess's 15th birthday was approaching, and for some reason, her mother decided to celebrate it this year, which baffled Jess. She did not like her birthday and believed that there was absolutely nothing to celebrate.

On the appointed day, Mom's few friends began to gather at the apartment. Mom shone among them. She did look good. Her new hairstyle, dress, and everything else practically screamed: look, I'm happy too, just like you! All those years of loneliness had clearly not been good for her. She was jealous of the home life of her colleagues and friends, unaware that things could be very different behind closed doors. It was obviously a revenge ball, the unfortunate woman getting back at everyone for years of fictional humiliations. Jess could not stand the sight. Every time her mom graciously passed a dish to a guest, Jess remembered the woman's face bent over her, the cruel grin and dishevelled hair. 'If they only knew who you really are,' Jess thought. When Nick appeared, her mother dragged Jess out from behind the table and into the hallway so he could wish her a happy birthday.

"Happy birthday, Jess," Nick said, handing the birthday girl a bouquet of daisies.

"Thank you," the girl replied without moving.

"Come one, honey, take the flowers," her mother urged.

Jess did as she was told. As soon as she drew near, Nick leaned forward to kiss her on the cheek, but she turned her head and the kiss accidentally landed on her lips. Jess pulled away in fright and glanced at her mother.

"I'm sorry, that was awkward," Nick simply laughed.

Mom laughed too, to Jess's relief.

The evening passed calmly, with no sign of what was to come. The guests gradually left, Jess was tidying up the remains of the feast, and Victoria went to see Nick off.

Mom returned quite soon. She entered quietly and went into the kitchen, where Jess was still washing the dishes, to pour herself a full glass of wine.

"Turn off the faucet!" Her mother snarled. There was no trace of her gracious manner at the party.

Jess obeyed. She knew what was coming next. It is true that children who are abused start to detect the subtlest signs of aggression in those around them.

"I knew you were a whore!"

"Mommy, why are you saying that?" Jess whispered softly.

"Shut up, you disgusting creature! Decided to steal Nick away from me, have you? They told me not to adopt you, that you were just like your mother. She's probably a slut like you."

Tears ran down Jess's cheeks.

"I'm going to teach you a lesson so that you keep your eyes to yourself!"

"Mommy! It wasn't me. Please, please don't." The girl begged, but to no avail.

Victoria finished her wine in one gulp, jumped up from the chair, and rushed at Jess. She grabbed the girl by the hair with such force that she immediately knocked her to the floor. Victoria dragged her all over the apartment, kicking and punching her. It went on for so long that Jess ran out of breath and began to feel like she was suffocating. Only then did her mother leave her alone. Jess lay on the cold floor, strewn with clumps of her hair, with nothing but hate pounding in her skull.

She did not go to school for two weeks, her mother waiting for her scratches and bruises to fade. While her mother was at work, Jess began to go outside, wandering aimlessly around the streets. This was how she met Sean. He was much older than Jess and clearly had habits that she was familiar with from childhood. She would never have approached him herself, she was afraid of men, but he came up to her, speaking softly and making jokes. That was how their friendship began.

He was far from handsome, but God had blessed him with a different gift, namely an excellent sense of humour. Jess had a lot of fun with him. The funniest thing was that he didn't shy away from making jokes about himself and his appearance. He said things like, "When I joke about my shortcomings first, I rob others of the opportunity to insult me. I don't care how I look, but I don't let people laugh at me, I laugh myself. That's the way it is, kiddo."

He was Jess's first friend, even though he was not the kind of friend her mother would want for her. Jess did not tell her mother or anyone else about him, but she suddenly felt motivated to change things after befriending him. Sean had unknowingly breathed life into Jess. For some reason, she began to pay more attention to her appearance, and learned to create fancy braids. Of course, she started skipping school and hung out at Sean's apartment all day. His mom did not mind Jess. She was busy with her own life and only made sure that her son was fed. She had no idea about his terrible habits. Every time Jess left their apartment, she thought about motherhood and what it meant. Her own upbringing was based on wordless obedience. Jess could not understand the purpose of this authoritarianism and what her mother was trying to achieve. On the other hand, Sean's relationship with his mother was just as bad. Yes, nobody beat the boy and he had enough to eat, but his mother had no clue about what was going on inside his head or his soul.

Really, what was parenting? Was it being a neighbour, friend, mentor, or jailer? Such thoughts led her to the conclusion that she would never have children, because she had no idea what to do with them and what they needed to be happy. She did not know how to love because no one had ever loved her. Plus, bringing children into this crazy world seemed like utter madness. She had no desire to follow in the footsteps of her own parents.

Christmas drew near. A wonderful time filled with the scent of cinnamon, citrus and approaching magic. Mom had broken up with Nick by this time and had become completely deranged. She drank often and would instantly become aggressive. Harsh even when she was sober, she lost all semblance of humanity once she became drunk. Victoria would invariably beat Jess when she was drunk. This had become a habit. While Jess could not defend herself previously, she now began to stand up for herself. The mother, seeing that beatings no longer scared her daughter, invented a new way to humiliate her.

"Take off everything I bought you!" Mom would scream, pulling off Jess's sweater, jeans, and underwear. "Get out of here, devil's spawn. You can leave in what you came in!"

Victoria would push her naked daughter out the door, knowing the unbearable shame it caused her. Jess would curl into a ball on the floor and sob uncontrollably. Meanwhile, her mother would kick her in this position. No, this could not go on any longer.

On New Year's Eve, Jess, who had not slept all night, quietly got out of bed, and prepared to do what she had long been planning. She took out a small bottle of sleeping pills, recently stolen from her mother's makeup bag. She opened it and hesitated. She was scared.

"Don't think," she ordered herself, and began to swallow the pills one by one. When the bottle was almost empty, Jess considered how she was feeling. Nothing was happening so far. After 10-15 minutes, she felt abruptly dizzy, and her stomach cramped with pain.

"Oh my God, what have I done?" Jess wailed. "Is this really the end? Am I going to die, and nothing will ever happen to me again? No, no, no! Dear God, please save me. Forgive me, I don't want to die!"

Jess wanted to run to the bathroom, but her body felt sluggish. She made it to the bathroom somehow and tried to make herself vomit. It did not work. Taking a toothbrush and sticking it as far back as possible, she managed to partially empty her stomach. Suddenly, her mother burst into the bathroom.

"Why can't you let me sleep on my day off?"

"I don't feel well," Jess said weakly.

"Ugh," Mom grimaced. "Clean up this mess once you're done."

Jess slept through the day. She woke up as the sun was setting, touched her body and cried. Tears of joy rolled down her cheeks. She thanked God that he did not take her away and promised never to do anything like this again. She would live no matter what. She would live!

Mom, thinking that her daughter was sick, let her rest for a couple of days and did not touch her. This gave Jess the chance to consider her future. She wanted to finish school as soon as possible, go to university and make her way in the world. She decided not to miss another day of school. As always, life had different plans.

It all happened on her mother's birthday. Victoria did not go to work that morning, and when she entered the kitchen, looking dishevelled, the first thing she did was open a bottle of whisky. She sat quietly by the window, deep in thought. This was not like her at all. Jess was alarmed by her mother's behaviour. She was less frightened of the inevitable beating than of Victoria's appearance. There was no life in her at all. Jess thought that her mother might be going crazy. Dark thoughts raced through her head while she was at school. She was afraid of everything. Arriving home in the late afternoon, Jess found her mother seated in the same place.

"Jess!" the woman called.

"I'm here," Jess replied, cautiously entering the kitchen.

"I can't live with you any longer," Victoria said, staring out the window. "You have to leave. I didn't just fail to love you, I hate you with every fibre of my being. I hate myself too. I'm living in hell. I don't want the sin of beating you to death one day. You don't know this, but I used to be a completely different person. I loved a man, and he loved me. For the first time in my life, someone truly loved me for simply being me, and not for any achievements or deeds. I thought that I'd found my happiness, but it was taken away in a single day. It ruined my life, it ruined me and, eventually, I started to destroy the lives of others, unaware that I was turning into the very person who had stolen my future. I became an exact copy of my mother. How many more lives must be destroyed? Someone has to break this vicious circle. Could I have done things differently? I don't know. I've thought about the past so many times, trying to find a solution, but I end up in the same place each time. Maybe I should have left my mother, but if you only knew how afraid I was of her! Although you do know. You need to leave right now. Pack your things and take the money on the shelf. There's not much there, $60, but it should be enough for the first little while."

Jess stood staring at her mother in disbelief. She could not process what was happening. On the one hand, she wanted to leave this cruel woman, but on the other hand, she suddenly felt sorry for her. Jess began to cry, for her mother and for herself. She felt sorry for herself because she had absolutely nowhere to go.

"Mom," Jess said softly.

"I'm not your mom, and I never was. We're done."

Jess had no choice but to do what Victoria said. She knew that if she did not leave now, she would leave anyway, but with bruises. Throwing her things into two bags and hiding the money in her jacket pocket, Jess left home.

The sun had set, and it was particularly cold and uninviting. Jess glanced up at the sky and her heart sank. She felt incredibly alone and abandoned. Where could she go? What should she do next? Even if she found a place to sleep for tonight, what about tomorrow? She had few options. Jess could go either to her school friend or to her grandmother. Jess imagined going over to her friend's house and having to explain why she was outside alone, clutching bags of clothes. She would have to fake a smile, keep herself together, and endure the humiliating sympathy of the other girl's parents. Her grandmother would rant about how bad her mother was and how bad Jess was, but at least she could remain silent and not waste her energy on meaningless games. Things unfolded exactly as expected at her grandmother's house.

"I won't be responsible for Victoria's decisions. She dragged you in, didn't she? You can stay here tonight, but you should look for another place tomorrow. This isn't a hotel. If I'd been the one talking to her, I'd have given her a piece of my mind! To drag a strange girl home without asking me, not even raise her properly, and then dump her on my lap!"

Grandma was in a state by this point. Fortunately, Jess was

allowed to withdraw to her room, where it was harder to hear her grandmother's words. The girl thought that she would never fall asleep. It felt like she would search for a solution all night, but her young body sought refuge in sleep, which was the best solution for today.

The house was quiet the next morning. Grandma had gone out, so Jess had time to eat a hearty breakfast and clean herself up. She knew that she would not be allowed to stay here tonight, so she had to prepare for anything. Taking a bottle of water and a couple of bread rolls with her, Jess sighed heavily and left the apartment.

Jess wandered the streets but could think of nothing better than to go and stay with her school friend. As she passed her mother's house, she glanced up at the windows. Mom wasn't there. For a moment, doubt crept into her mind about her mother's state, and she grew alarmed.

"What if she did something to herself?" Jess wondered. Although her inner voice insisted that such a woman was incapable of suicide, her heart prevailed. Jess entered the building, climbed the stairs to the right floor, and put her ear to the door. Her mother's voice, utterly calm, could be heard on the other side. Jess realised that she was talking to Nick and felt so hurt! Anger, rage, and hatred boiled up inside her.

'First you took me away from my sisters, deprived me of my freedom and my own opinions. You've maimed my body and soul, and now, after casting me out, you're going to live as if nothing had happened!'

Jess clenched her fists and rang the doorbell. She prepared to spit out the monologue stuck in her throat at the woman it was meant for. But as soon as she heard the shuffling steps on the other side of the door, Jess felt terrified again, and raced up the stairs to the floor above. Her Mom opened the door, and seeing no one there, went back inside.

Jess stood outside the neighbour's door for a long time before snapping out of her daze. She left the apartment building, slamming the door behind her. A quick change of plans and she headed for the familiar courtyard. She rang the bell when she reached the apartment.

"Sean's not home," his mother said, opening the door.

"I know, he said to wait for him in his room," Jess lied.

"Well, come in then."

Sean's mom clearly was not happy about the arrival of an unexpected guest. She was especially confused by the bags of clothing Jess held in her arms.

Entering Sean's room, Jess first hid her clothes in the closet and, sitting on the sofa, began to consider what she was going to say to her friend. When Sean returned home from work, he did not immediately go to his room. He had a long dinner, and then took a shower, so that Jess was at her wit's end by the time he finally entered the bedroom.

"Surprise!" she exclaimed.

"What are you doing here?" Sean asked, puzzled.

"I had a fight with my mom," Jess lied again. "Anyway, can I stay with you for a while? I would stay with my grandmother, but she has all these relatives staying over at the moment..."

"Um, I don't even know what to say."

"I won't stay for long. I'll try to make up with my mom as soon as possible. I'll just stay here for 5-7 days."

"Alright," Sean agreed, "but you'll have to sleep in my bed. There's nowhere else."

"I won't bother you," Jess exhaled.

If Jess had known that 5-7 days would turn into several long and painful years, would she have stayed with Sean? It is difficult to say.

Things were fine at first. Jess went to school, and then ran home to cook for the family. Sean's mother did not mind having a free maid. Jess, aware that she could be thrown out at any moment, tried to curry favour as much as possible. She and Sean lived like good friends, even though they slept in the same bed. The guy was cautious and did not show any interest in Jess. They watched movies together in the evenings and Jess gradually began to develop feelings for her friend. She often rested her head on his shoulder and occasionally held his hand. She still did not find him attractive, on the contrary, but living side by side with him, she stopped noticing his obvious flaws. Jess was grateful to Sean for taking her in, and it was this gratitude that led to what happened next.

The first time they had sex was awful, and so were all the subsequent times. It was only much later than Jess realized how clueless Sean was when it came to intimacy. He did not think about her at all and was like an animal, leaving behind only a sense of disappointment. Yes, she had certainly imagined it differently.

After nine months of living together, Jess began to notice certain changes in Sean. He had grown tired of her. While she could previously defuse his occasional aggressive outbursts, this now became impossible. Sean began to use illegal substances more often when hanging out with his friends, which never leads to anything good. His already unstable mental state took a turn for the worse. He would apologise the next morning, but that did not change the fact that he started hitting Jess, and then kicking her out of the house. Events were repeating themselves.

Worst of all, she thought that she loved him, so when she went to stay with a school friend after another fight, she waited for him to take her back. The relationship quickly turned abusive. The awful thing was that she did not even realise it and blamed herself, not him, for what was happening. She kept thinking that she should not have said this or that, and that she should just stay silent when he got angry. What a fool she was!

When Jess finally scraped through the final year of school, she learned both that she was pregnant and that her mother had unexpectedly died. It turned out that Victoria had breast cancer, which she had known about, yet she had refused treatment. Jess's grandmother handed her the farewell letter, still cursing her deceased and miserable daughter.

"Jess!

I'm writing you a farewell letter, a letter that can't atone for my sins. I've told you the story of my life, and now I'll tell you the story of my death. Once I was a girl like you, and I believed in fairy tales. My fairy tale could have easily become reality if I'd fought for it. But I was scared. I've done nothing that I could have or wanted to do. I'm dying, and it's my own fault. All my life, I've been angry at my mother, angry at fate, angry at myself, my colleagues, work, and friends. The priest says that it was the resentment, lodged like a splinter in my soul, that made me sick. Perhaps he's right. I'm sorry that I adopted you back then. I didn't think I'd be such a bad mother. I had no other parenting role models, so I followed a familiar path that turned out to be utterly wrong. I hope I haven't broken your spirit like my mother once broke mine. Try to be happy.

Forgive me,

Your mom.

P.S. The bank will repossess the apartment, so you should go and live with your grandmother, she will take you in.

I've also left you some money. It'll be enough for a deposit on your own home. You can take it when you turn 21."

Jess's heart shattered into pieces. It was unbearable to think that Victoria Meadow never ended up living like a queen, and that she had died so stupidly. Her poor, poor mother! Jess could not control her sobs and forgave her mother for all that she had done wrong.

That night, Jess woke up with a sharp pain in her lower abdomen. She tried not to scream, patiently waiting for the pain to stop. She didn't want to wake Sean, after all, he had to get up at 6 a.m. every day and go to work without breakfast. She felt sorry for him, but not for herself. The pain did not subside and had reached its peak by 9 a.m. Jess finally decided to call an ambulance. She did not remember how she ended up in the vehicle and struggled to remember what the doctor said. There was only a roar in her head and a single sentence, "We will try to save your child."

She had infusions and injections all day, and the pain slowly receded. Waking up at night from a dream, Jess gazed out the window, remembering the past day. An unusually bright moon hung outside the window, distracting Jess from her thoughts. To her surprise, she slipped out of bed and began to pray, "Please save my child's life. I beg you. I'll do whatever you ask. Please help me."

She knelt for a long time, believing that this prayer would work. It did. The baby remained in her womb, and Jess was over the moon with happiness. She already loved it. Sean seemed to share her joy on the phone, but it later turned out that he partied with friends and beautiful girls while Jess fought for their child's life. He did not visit her once in hospital.

When the truth came out, including all the sordid details, she packed her things and left Sean's home. She lived with her grandmother for almost the entire pregnancy. Of course, Sean did not want to let her go just like that. He wanted the freedom to do whatever he liked, but he also wanted his faithful dog Jess to meet him at the door. He told her all sorts of lies to get her to come back. He talked about their happy family, about the business he would open when he saved up some money, about how they would buy a house and get a dog. This Jess's weak spot since she always wanted to have a real family. Yes, she came back.

On a rainy autumn night, she gave birth to a boy, whom they named Edwin. Jess picked up the sweet-smelling baby, wrapped in a blanket with kittens on it. To her surprise, he immediately smiled at her, or maybe she simply imagined it. She gazed at him and couldn't believe that she was now a mother, and finally had someone to love. Jess did not feel overwhelming love for this little lump yet, but she listened to her feelings.

That night, she was struck by the inhuman torments that bring a new person into this world. Her own mother had experienced the same pain and suffering. How had she cared so little about the miracle of creation? Jess gazed into the small, wrinkled face and promised her son that she would forever break the vicious circle of cruelty she had experienced.

"I'll love you with all my heart. I'll do everything in my power to make you happy. I'm not going to tell you to "get out," I won't say a single nasty word to you. I'll take care of you, and when I get old, you'll take care of me."

Cradling the fragile body, she whispered words of gratitude to heaven.

Life was very different once Edwin was born. Sean quickly grew tired of the baby, his screams, smells, and so on. Sean's mother was also unsupportive. She disliked that there was less and less room in the apartment. This is not what she had wanted for her son. The atmosphere grew more tense over time. Sean's mother poured poison into Sean's ear, unaware of what this would lead to. He began to use more and was in a drug-addled state more often. One day, when the baby was about 3 months old, Sean lost all control of himself. He got home, lay down on the sofa, turned the music on full blast, and buried his face in the pillow. The music was quickly cut off.

"You're going to wake the baby," Jess said, rushing into the room. She held a ladle with which she had been stirring soup.

Sean leaped up and, snatching the aluminium ladle from Jess's hands, began to violently beat her with it. She did not scream at first, afraid to wake the child, but when she realized that he might kill her, she screamed as loudly as she could. This enraged her tormentor even more. He started slapping her across the face and tearing her clothes. Luckily, Sean's mother was home at the time. She ran into the room and put a stop to the beating. When she saw that Jess was bleeding, the woman only said, "Don't call an ambulance!" Sean's mother knew that Sean would get in trouble for this, but she didn't care about what happened to Jess.

Nevertheless, Jess called an ambulance. The doctors arrived in 4 minutes, and while they were there, Jess packed up her things, picked up the crying Edwin, and left Sean's apartment forever.

At the hospital, they discovered that Jess had multiple head wounds and a concussion, but nothing life-threatening. The doctors convinced her to report Sean to the police, which allowed her to obtain a restraining order against him.

Jess was forced to ask her grandmother to shelter her again. She was willing to beg and do all the hard work, just so Edwin had a roof over his head. Strangely enough, Grandma let her back in. The girl noticed that the callous woman had softened during her absence. Perhaps she had looked at her life with fresh eyes.

"What would you know," Grandma said, "history repeats itself. A pity that last time I didn't accept the baby but forced her to commit a murder."

Jess didn't say anything, puzzled.

"You need to find a job," Grandma continued, "I'll look after the boy."

Jess found a job. Unfortunately, without education or experience, she could only get a job as a store cleaner. The work was exhausting and didn't bring much money, but it was better than nothing. A child meant constant expenses, and the social benefits Jess received were not enough.

One pay day, Jess left the bank, but did not go home immediately. She wandered the streets, looking at all the new buildings in her home suburb.

"Wow, there are so many offices next to us," Jess marvelled, having never noticed this before. Lately, she constantly thought about where to get more money. She woke up and fell asleep with this thought. It is hard to live when you are barely surviving. Nothing pleases you and life seems drab and grey.

"So many employees, yet not a single cafe," Jess noted.

Suddenly, an idea popped into her head. What if she cooked healthy, home-made food and delivered it to the offices? Jess carried the idea around inside her head for several days, consumed by a mixture of hope and fear. One day, she sat down at the table and sketched out a varied menu for 5 working days. Jess calculated the cost of the dishes, and, in the best-case scenario, the profit would be pretty good. In the future, it would allow her to hire assistants, scale up the business, and perhaps help other moms on maternity leave.

"Aren't you getting carried away?" She laughed at herself yet put her plan into action.

After finding out the phone numbers of all the companies in the area, she began calling each one to offer her services. To her great disappointment, every single company declined. This was deeply upsetting, but Jess would not give up so easily. After printing out a sample menu, she went in person, leaving a brochure in each office. This did not work either. Despite the setback, Jess still cooked 15 servings and went to the office centre with Edwin. The guard let her in when she explained that she had brought hot lunches. At first, she was a little embarrassed to open her mouth and say, look, I cook healthy and delicious meals, but by the fifth office, she could calmly repeat the phrase she had memorized. Jess would never forget the first woman who bought a meal from her out of pity. From now on, this woman would regularly order her lunches from Jess. Moreover, she would encourage her entire office to do this. But that would come later. In the meantime, Jess sold only one lunch and returned home completely crushed. All week, both she and her grandmother had to eat healthy meat patties, mashed potatoes and vegetable salad for breakfast, lunch, and dinner. On Friday, Jess received an email from the woman in the office.

Dear Miss Jessica,

I hope you are doing well. I wanted to express my thanks for the wonderful lunch I had on Monday. I wanted to tell you that it was delicious. Please deliver 35 hot lunches next Monday. Awaiting your reply.

Sincerely,

Angeline

Jess stared at the screen and could not believe her luck. It felt like tremendous success. She immediately replied to Angeline, thanked her profusely, and promised to be there at lunchtime on Monday.

Thus began a new chapter in her life. Jess barely slept, working tirelessly. She counted every penny and did not give up her job as a cleaner. Everything she earned, she brought home for the family. Edwin slowly grew and was the apple of Jess's eye. She did everything for him, she lived for him. By her son's first birthday, Jess had even saved up some money and threw a party, with guests, a cake and presents. For some reason, she cried a lot that day.

As always happens, before Jess had overcome her past difficulties, fate had new ones in store for her. First, her grandmother began to experience serious health problems. She was quite old and, unfortunately, developed dementia. The disease began quite innocuously but progressed rapidly and soon became impossible to manage. Although Jess hated the thought of it, Grandma had to be placed in an aged care home. When Jess came to visit her for the first time, she suddenly took a good look at her familiar stranger.

"I'm here," Jess said softly, sitting on the edge of the bed beside the motionless body. "What's wrong?"

"I don't like it here," Grandma whispered. "They seem nice, but I want to go home, I want to see Victoria and Arnold."

Jess realized that the woman was confused.

"Grandma, we'll visit Victoria later. They're not here."

"Who are you?"

"I'm Jess, your granddaughter."

"Granddaughter? How strange, I remember that it was a boy when I sent Victoria to the doctor," she suddenly stopped and starting sobbing. The nurse came in and injected the woman with a sedative, and Jess left the room after she fell asleep.

Along the way, the girl carefully looked around the aged care home once again. It was a nice place, cosy and warm, but it wasn't home. Jess thought that she should not have left her grandmother here and decided to take her back the very next weekend. She was forced to hire a carer, with her neighbour agreeing to work part-time. This put a serious dent in the budget, but now both Edwin and grandmother were being looked after. The problem again highlighted the Jess's lack of money.

One evening, Jess came home, collapsed on the sofa, and could not get up for a long time. She could hear Edwin crying in the next room, and her grandmother's frantic shouting coming from above, but this did not elicit a reaction. She was tired. She was so tired that she wanted nothing more than peace and quiet. She did not even care about Edwin right now. Terrible images of everyone's deaths floated through her mind. Jess mistakenly believed that she could only find peace in death. Edwin's screams became more insistent. She forced herself to stand up through sheer force of will.

"What is it, little one?" she said, entering the child's room to find him crimson from crying. "Chiara is looking after Grandma and doesn't come to you? What would you like? Are you hungry?"

After feeding and calming the boy down, she went upstairs. "Grandma, are you okay?" Jess asked, opening the door.

"Oh, Jess, she's not in a good mood today. She won't let me wash her," Chiara answered for her grandmother.

"What would I do without you, my dear Chiara? Thank you so much."

"Oh, it's nothing. Alright, I'll leave you to it. Good night, Mrs. Meadow," the woman said and left the room.

"What's the matter, Gran? She's trying to help you by looking after you."

"She prays a hundred times a day, muttering something in her own language."

"So what? What's wrong with a person believing in God? You believe in him too."

"Her God is the wrong God."

"Stop it, Gran. You're an adult and there's a lot I'd like to say to you, but I don't want to upset you by telling the unpleasant truth. Chiara is a good person. She looks after you for a pittance since I pay her almost nothing. You should be grateful. Do you understand? Can you imagine what kind of world we'd live in if everyone was a little kinder? Oh, forget it! I'll turn the TV on low for you, so try to fall asleep."

Jess covered the old woman with a blanket and left the room with a heavy sigh. The thought that some people would never change, even when they had one foot in the grave, made her shrivel inside.

The alarm clock went off at 5 a.m. as always, so it was back to the grind. Although life was hard, Jess still thanked God for every new day as she rose from bed.

"I'm Jess Meadow and only good things happen in my life," she repeated her daily mantra.

The lunches were usually ready by 9 a.m., and then Jess would start making breakfast for her family. She first fed Edwin, then her grandmother, and only then did she have breakfast. She had lost a lot of weight over the past year and weighed only 49 kilograms. And she looked terrible, despite her young age.

The day went better than the last, because sweet Angeline had placed a big order for the weekend, which promised great profits. It meant Jess could buy new clothes for Edwin and Grandma.

"Tom's got a promotion," Ange said, grinning broadly. "The party is scheduled for Sunday at 4:00 p.m. And I thought, who better than Jess to prepare a party menu? You've organized something like this before, right?"

"Of course!" Jess lied. "What exactly are you after?"

"I don't know, the usual, I guess. Some snacks, canapes and so on. Plus, we need a hot lunch with meat and potatoes. Oh, and salads."

"No problem. I'll e-mail you the menu today before 5."

"Awesome!"

As Jess was leaving the office, she accidentally bumped into a young woman.

"Hey! Careful!"

"Sorry, I didn't mean to run into you. Are you hurt?"

"Jess?!" The young woman asked in surprise, her face breaking into a smile.

It took Jess a few moments to realize that this beautiful stranger was Helen, her former classmate.

"It's Helen!" the girl confirmed. "Don't you remember me?"

It was hard to recognize Helen in this well-groomed, smartly dressed young woman. She had grown taller since school and was at least a head taller than Jess. Her golden hair fell in glossy curls over her shoulders, and her eyes shone like emeralds. She exuded health and success.

"We haven't seen each other in a million years. How are you? I'd heard that you left town."

"No, no. I'm still here," Jess mumbled. She felt awkward beside Helen. She abruptly saw herself through the other girl's eyes and realised how unkempt she looked. "How are you doing? You look great."

"Oh, thank you. I'm well. I'm going to see my fiancé to discuss our wedding."

"You're getting married? Congratulations."

"Yes, check out the ring!" Helen shoved the ring right under Jess's nose.

"It's beautiful. Congratulations once again!"

"And how are you? Are you studying or working?"

"I'm working," Jess answered the last question, sidestepping the question of study, which was a sore spot for her. "You?"

"I'm studying. Medicine. I'm going to help people."

"That's wonderful. Listen, I must run, sorry. Congratulations once again. See you!"

Jess hugged her goodbye and hurried to the exit. The elevator didn't come for a long time, and all the while, Helen stared at Jess. Unable to stand her classmate's gaze, Jess waved and hurried down the stairs. She practically ran of the business centre, feeling utterly humiliated. Walking along a disgusting road in a disgusting city, as she thought, she kept berating herself.

"You're such a loser!" Jess told herself. "Helen's a doctor, while you're nobody! You've always been a nobody, and you'll die a nobody. Why, why am I so unlucky in life? What did I do wrong? God, I really hate you sometimes!"

Jess came home feeling distressed and her state affected the whole household. Edwin was crying, as always, and instead of calming him down, she yelled at him at the top of her voice. He gazed at her with his innocent eyes, big tears rolled down his pink cheeks. Jess felt ashamed and, falling to her knees, hugged her son.

"I'm sorry, I'm sorry," Jess kept saying. "It's not your fault. Sorry."

She thought a lot about her life over the next few days. She remembered that, as a child, she dreamed of being something more than what she was today. Jess did not shift the blame for her life onto her own parents or her foster mother. She took responsibility for what was happening and blamed only herself. Admitting your mistakes, as they say, is a good start. The only thing Jess knew was that she had to urgently change something in her life. She stopped her lunch business and quit her cleaning job. Her 21st birthday was drawing nearer, and she needed a business in which she could invest her inheritance, and which could support her family financially.

She wandered the streets and stared at the shop windows, as if she could find instructions for a happy life in there.

"What do people need?" Jess asked herself. "Everything has already been invented long ago. How do I create something that people need in the modern world, full of absolutely everything and more? Oh, don't forget that you're also utterly incompetent! You can't do anything except wash floors."

Nevertheless, passing by a bookshop one day, she saw something that shook her to the core. Two sad yellow eyes stared at her from the cover of a book by an author she did not know. These eyes looked alive and seemed to gaze into her very soul. Jess stared at them and felt as if these eyes understood her and felt everything that she felt. When she came home, she had a strange feeling.

"How do you make such toy eyes?" she wondered. "What are they made of?"

The question motivated her to seek answers. It turned out that there was a lot she did not know. There were so many different children's toys! How had she never noticed this before?

This was not important, though. There was a drive inside her, but she had no idea what it would lead to.

"Grandma, do you think I could learn how to sew?" Jess asked, bringing a spoonful of porridge to her grandmother's mouth.

"Probably," Grandma replied indifferently.

"Can you sew?"

"Yes, why?"

"Who taught you?"

"My mother."

"And what did you make?"

"Everything, I guess. Dresses, skirts, suits. We didn't have much money for beautiful clothes, so we had to make it ourselves."

"Do you have a sewing machine?"

"I used to keep it in the basement, I'm not sure. The last time I sewed something was when Victoria went to prom. Why doesn't she visit me?"

Grandma had such episodes every day, but she remained alert most of the time.

"She went away, Gran. Don't worry about it."

"Where could she have gone? Good-for-nothing slag! And me? Am I supposed to look after her child again?"

Jess, who was used to this sort of talk, did not say anything. She had more important things to think about. As soon as Chiara arrived, she went down to the basement and tried to find the sewing machine. It was hard to find anything among the piles of junk, so she had to clean the whole place.

"If you want to find something, sort out the mess," Jess repeated this like a mantra.

A couple of hours later, the junk had been taken to landfill, the useful items were neatly arranged, and the sewing machine had been found and placed on the table. Even though the machine was old, it sewed perfectly. All night, Jess practised various stitches and tried to sew at least a handkerchief. She scribbled things in her notebook, noting the smallest things. A week later, the basement was littered with patterns, threads, and drawings.

By the time she received her inheritance, Jess had a clear plan of action and the information necessary to start her business. After cashing in the cheque, she stepped outside and took a deep breath. Jess was buoyed by the success she was sure was coming, and also felt incredibly grateful to her departed mother.

When Jess returned home, she immediately placed a large order of supply materials for her products. She could already picture the finished delicate soft toy, with large acrylic eyes and long eyelashes. Her toy dragon would definitely have a heart, and this heart would warm any child. For some reason, she was certain that things would work out, although neither her grandmother nor Chiara supported the idea.

"Who would want these stuffed animals?" the old woman asked. "They'll only collect dust and cause allergies."

"One, I checked the material and it's hypoallergenic. Two, it will be a friend for those who have no friends."

"Oh, Jess. You shouldn't have wasted nearly all your mom's money on this nonsense. You should have left it in savings."

"We have enough to live on for the next 5-6 months, Gran. Trust me."

Grandma only shook her head. Perhaps, deep down, Jess

agreed with the older woman's common sense and wanted to leave the money untouched, but for the first time in her life, the desire for change overcame the voice of reason. Something was driving her forward, which meant it was worth the risk.

After receiving a huge box with her order, Jess began to create the patterns. She had practised with scrap materials and understood how sewing worked. Artificial fur turned out to be a little harder to sew than ordinary fabrics, but she got used to it.

Then came the sleepless days and nights. During the day, Jess cut, sewed, made toy eyes out of resign, and glued eyelashes to them. At night, she ran through sales options in her head. She needed advertising, but there was no money left for it. Jess reassured herself that she would definitely come up with something, and only then fell asleep. But in the morning, she awoke with anxiety, which became her constant companion Yes, she had a backup plan since she could return to cooking lunches, but it was not enough.

The first batch of toys was ready by November. The baby dragons looked incredible. Each had soft fur, shiny eyes, and a heart with a delicate strawberry aroma. But this wasn't all. Each one sat in a beautiful box shaped like a house, which Jess had designed and then glued by hand. A lot of work had gone into these toys. Jess had thought things through to the smallest detail. She considered what she would have wanted as a child, and what any child would want.

Jess locked herself in her room for several days before going to knock on doors. She could neither eat nor sleep and thought about only one thing: how to force herself to leave the house and persuade at least one store owner to sell her goods. She knew that she would have to hear hundreds of no's before receiving a single yes. This turned out to be the case. Every store owner already had trusted suppliers, and they were dubious about Jess's toys since it was much cheaper to import them from another country. They did not want the hassle of helping an unknown local manufacturer.

Every day, Jess returned home with nothing, collapsed on the bed, and cried. There was enough money left for two months, and she still had no orders.

"If I take the money for December and use it for ads, we will have nothing to live on. What if the ads don't work?" She wondered. "But what if they work? What should I do? What should I do?"

Despite her fear, she took the last desperate step and dipped into their December savings. The next week, photos of her little dragons appeared in the city newspaper, and the long-awaited phone call came a couple of days later.

"Good afternoon! I'm calling about the soft toys."

"Hello, this is Jessica speaking."

"I represent Miss N. You've probably heard of her?"

Jess's heart did a somersault. Of course, she had heard the name, read about her, and seen her on TV. Miss N was an important figure. She seemed to do so many helpful and kind things for others. Trying to calm the beating of her heart, Jess returned to the conversation.

"Yes, of course I have."

"We're planning a promotional tour and we'd like to order a large batch of toys. Do you have 120 pieces in stock?"

Jess had about 100, but she could make another 20 in a couple of days. "Yes," she replied without hesitation.

"Excellent. When can you deliver the order?"

"The day after tomorrow, I think. Please text me your email address, I'll create the purchase order and list the full price there."

"Certainly. We'll be waiting for you at noon. I'll include the address in the email."

Jess hung up the phone and rushed around the room. She did not know what to do with herself, she was ready to burst with joy. Could it be that a person like Miss N. was ordering toys from a nobody like Jess? This could be a great start! Maybe the store owners will change their mind once they learn that a celebrity bought Jess's creations?

On the appointed day, Jess hired a small pickup truck, loaded 120 boxes into it and headed to the specified address. When Jess arrived at an enormous mansion, she could not bring herself to get out of the car for a long time. Smoothing her hair and glancing in the mirror, she opened the car door and headed for the entrance.

"Oh, you must be Jessica?" Said Miss N.'s assistant as he opened the door.

"Yes. Hello."

"I appreciate your punctuality. I'll ask someone to unload this, so please wait here."

"I can do it myself."

"Even better!"

While Jess was unloading the toys, Miss N. descended the staircase.

"Is this it?" she asked, ignoring the young woman.

"Yes, that's it," Jess replied as she entered. "It's lovely to meet you."

"Uh-huh," Miss N. grunted unkindly.

Jess drove back with a sinking feeling. How different was the television version of Miss N. from the real one. There was none of the lightness or kindness that she broadcast to the world. Jess had a sense of foreboding. How upsetting that a person admired by millions, including her, had turned out to be so different. What worried her most was that they had not paid for the toys, not even a part payment.

Many days passed since the order had been delivered, yet Jess did not receive a cheque or a bank transfer. She called Miss N.'s assistant many times. At first, he answered the phone and advised her wait, but then he stopped picking up the phone.

The house was a mess and so was Jess. There was almost no food left, and she had to ask Chiara to stop coming. It was becoming increasingly difficult to look after grandmother and Edwin, given that Jess was already exhausted.

Tired of waiting for payment, Jess gathered her courage and headed for Miss N.'s house. She had to take Edwin with her as Grandma was quite confused that day. No one opened the door for a long time, but she refused to leave the porch and continued to ring the bell. Finally, Miss N. herself opened the door. "What do you want?" she asked. "Why are you bothering me?"

"My name is Jess. I provided toys for your charity, and you promised to pay but I never received a cent."

"Ha, well, you weren't supposed to get anything!" The celebrity replied arrogantly.

Jess had not expected this. "What do you mean? We had

an agreement. I made an additional 20 toys especially for you. I gave you everything I had."

"Listen, girlie! You ought to get out of here and thank me for not filing a police report on you! You gave us bad toys and the kids developed an allergy!"

"That's impossible! The material is hypoallergenic!"

"That's what you think! If I say that they had an allergic reaction, then that's what happened. Look at her, she even brought her own child along! What, so I'd feel sorry for you? Like I'd fall for that!"

Tears welled up in Jess's eyes. She could not believe such a horrible turn of events. It was so unfair.

"Get off my property and don't call me again," Miss N. said and slammed the door in Jess's face.

Jess stood rooted to the spot for a long time. She could not move. She could not believe that this was the end.

"Mommy, are you crying?" Little Edwin asked.

"I am, baby."

"Don't cry, Mommy."

She tried to pull herself together on the way home. She could not bear the thought that this was the end. But most of all she could not understand how one human being could treat another this way. How could some people lose the last shred of decency? Or maybe they never had any at all?

Jess did not leave the house for the next few days, having lost all hope and motivation. She did not know how to keep living. The phone rang from time to time, but Jess did not have the strength to pick it up. When she went down to the basement and saw the empty boxes, leftover fabric and sewing machine, she wanted to burn it all. Anger boiled up in her, even hatred. Why were some rich people so greedy, she wondered? She thought that the point of money was to help others. She was no drunk, drug addict or slacker! She had made high-quality toys with her own two hands, her fingers covered in needle pricks, and her back aching from fatigue. Why had she been treated so dishonestly? She could not wrap her head around it.

With Christmas only a week away, Jess's phone started to ring more than usual. Having gathered herself and accepted what had happened, she answered the call.

"Hello! I'm calling about the dragons. We need seven."

"I'm sorry, they're not in stock at the moment."

"Oh, no! When will they be back? I'm going to see my nephews and I really wanted to give them something special."

"What's your name?"

"Taylor."

"It's nice to meet you, Taylor. I'm Jess. I'll see what we have left and call you back in a couple of hours," Jess replied.

Something in the caller's voice struck a chord in Jess, so she went down to the basement to check how much fabric remained. There was enough left to make more than seven toys, so Jess decided to try again.

"Good evening, Taylor. We'll be able to fill the order. You can come by tomorrow evening and pay in cash. I'll send you the total cost in a text. Please confirm if you're happy with the amount."

"Wow, super, thanks Jess."

The following evening, a girl with short hair drove up to Jess's house. She exuded such energy and positivity that Jess could not help but be swept up in it.

"I thought it was a warehouse. Do you sew them yourself?"

"Yes, in the basement."

"Wow, I'd never have guessed. Listen, you've come up with a great idea. These eyes with the eyelashes are so unusual. My nephews are going to love them. It's strange that they're not in the stores."

"No one wanted to try selling them."

"Well then, you've got to come up with something!"

"Yes, I should," Jess replied sadly. "Well, happy holidays."

"Thank you," Taylor replied as she strode away, but her gaze lingered on Jess.

Jess had no idea that this would not be their last meeting. The next day, Taylor called her again. "Listen, who's in charge of sales in your business?"

"I am."

"No, that won't do. I have a suggestion. Seems to me that you're a good person, and so am I, so why don't we try running the business together? You'll sew the toys as before, and I'll sell them."

"I don't have any money to pay your salary, and there is almost no fabric left."

"What a shame. I couldn't sleep yesterday; I kept staring into the dragon's eyes and it just felt like it could understand me."

"That's right," Jess smiled.

"Okay, well, bye. Call me if anything changes."

After talking to Taylor, Jess's only thought was where to get more money. She was out of options. No one would give her a loan, and there was nothing left to sell.

Jess was cleaning her grandmother's room right before

New Year's Eve when her gaze fell on a jewellery box. Jess had never seen it before. Opening the box, she saw various pieces of jewellery, some of which were gold.

"Grandma, what's this?" Jess asked, holding up the box.

"These are gifts from Arnold," Grandma replied, her fingers running over the jewellery. "Victoria will get all this when she gets married, so you should put it back."

"Have you ever thought about selling any of them? Victoria won't need them anyway."

"Absolutely not! Put it back immediately!"

Even today, Jess remained ashamed of what she did back then. Taking her grandmother's jewellery and hiding the box, she pawned the contents, promising herself that she would buy it all back using her first profits. She now had money to buy a small amount of fabric and she immediately called Taylor. "Hi, it's Jess."

"Hello. How are you?"

"I'm fine, thanks. A new batch of toys will be ready tomorrow. I wanted to ask if we could make a deal?"

"About what?"

"I buy the materials and sew the toys, and you sell them. We split the profit 70/30. The difference will be pretty small once I deduct my expenses. We'll receive almost the same amount."

"So, what's the catch?"

"The catch is that I don't have any money to pay you yet."

Taylor laughed. "Interesting. It's a tempting offer," she replied with a touch of sarcasm. "But you know, I'll still say yes. I can see the potential. I can juggle this with my main job, so I'll come out on top either way."

This is how their business began. Taylor was an excellent promoter, and orders began to flow like a river. Jess even had to hire someone to help with production. By May, they were turning a profit, had officially registered a company, and her grandmother's jewellery was all back in its box. There was a lot of work, but it was joyful because Jess was on the up and up. A little later, they moved from the cramped basement into a small workshop and hired more workers. Jess paid them a decent salary as well as constant bonuses, because she knew better than anyone about the plight of women down on their luck.

Jess grew more confident as the money rolled in. She began to dress better and changed her hairstyle. Success suited her, but it did not go to head, and she continued to play an active role in production.

One late evening, Sean appeared on her doorstep. It was an unexpected and unpleasant surprise.

"What are you doing here?" Jess asked, opening the door.

"I came to visit my son."

Jess saw that he was on something. "You're not going to see him. His life is peaceful and should not be disturbed. Which is precisely what you've done for all these years."

"Don't tell me who I will or won't see! Keep talking like that and I'll take him away! We fed you and housed you for so many years, and this is the thanks we get? You owe us!"

"Oh, so you came for the money?" Jess responded calmly to his accusations.

"No, I just want to see my son."

"If you wanted to see your son, why did you take drugs? Have you been smoking something or what?"

"None of your damn business!"

"Give me a second," Jess said, closing the door.

A minute later, she came out onto the porch with a huge wrench in her hands. She swung it, her eyes burning with anger. "Now, listen here, you piece of shit! If you ever come here again, I'll kill you! I'll beat you until your ugly mug stops making any sounds. I'm not kidding! I won't hesitate to pay you back for everything you ever did to me. Do you hear me?"

It was the first time Sean had seen Jess in such a state and, backing away to the gate, he sobered up instantly. "Jess, what are you doing?" he asked.

"Get the hell out! Right now!" Jess screamed.

She never saw Sean again, but his appearance made her turn to lawyers and obtain sole custody of Edwin. She found an excellent lawyer, even though he worked in a small and unremarkable office. This was the first case he won for Jess. The second one would come much later.

"So, you want full custody, Miss Meadow? Was the child's father involved in his upbringing?"

"No, Mr. Gable. I can provide evidence: receipts, kindergarten payments, etc."

"Yes, we will attach it to the case file. I'll gather all the documents so that the case is decided quickly. By the way, you can call me Allan."

"It's not a very common name."

"Yes, that's true. I was named after my father."

Allan turned out to be a very pleasant person. He exuded calm, yet there was a sense of inner strength in him too. He seemed like a person you could rely on in any situation. He kept his promise regarding a quick decision and Jess received sole custody of her son in a short amount of time.

Now that Jess's life was sufficiently stable, she began to think about a second child. She wanted to bestow her love on someone else. Her desire grew stronger by the day, and so she went to the very place she had once been taken from. The director had changed, of course, and so had the rules. For some reason, the new management were reluctant to let single women adopt children, as if having a man was an indicator of stability. The new director listened carefully to Jess and said, "Miss Meadow, we can review your application, but it will take you a long time to gather the necessary documents."

Jess was not worried about that, since she already knew the person who could help her.

"I'll gather everything you require and even more. Look, how many children do you have? At least one of them could gain a loving mother this way."

"We'll still need to check that! Do you have any idea how many people come to us? No? Some of them adopt children and then don't keep their promises."

"I went through precisely what you're talking about. I already have a child. I just thought I could help someone else and give them a chance in life."

"I understand. You seem like a decent woman, so I'll ask my assistant to place you in the queue, and we'll see how things go. The committee makes the decision."

Seven months later, Jess led a skinny girl down the street. She was still frightened, like Jess once was, and showed no affection for her "new mother".

The girl's name was Roberta. She was 8 years old when

she came to live with Jess. She was a quiet, shy, and reserved child. She was not familiar with human cruelty but knew the bitterness of loss. Roberta's parents had adored her and given her with everything they could. Alas, their lives were cut short by an accident. Roberta could not get used to her new family for a long time, despite their efforts. Jess decided not to put pressure on Berta and simply gave her what she had in abundance, namely love, warmth and care. She said, "I know that I will never become your mother, because you already have a mother. She lives in your heart, and she looks down on you from heaven. But I can be your friend; I can help you when you need me to and keep you safe."

Roberta spoke little at first, although she obediently went to school and cleaned up her room. Gradually, her heart began to thaw thanks to the kindness of her new family, and she began to repay them with the same. She got along well with Edwin too. And so, life went on.

Jess worked tirelessly, determined to provide the best for those she was responsible for. One day, a local newspaper came to interview her about her success. Everyone saw the interview, including people who were most unwelcome.

One cold winter day, as the children were building a snowman on the lawn, they were approached by a woman of dubious appearance.

"Hello," she said. "Does Jess Meadow live here?"

Berta looked at the woman suspiciously and, grabbing Edwin by the scruff of the neck, hurried into the house.

"Jessica, there's a woman out there!" The girl shrieked as she entered.

"What woman?"

"I don't know. She's asking about you. I'm scared."

"Don't worry, honey. I'll sort it out."

Jess went out on the porch and stared at the stranger for a long time before realising who she was. It was hard to recognize the woman who had given birth to her in this poorly dressed, thin and emaciated figure.

"Hello," Jess said, "I didn't expect to see you here."

Once upon a time, Jess thought that if she ever saw her mother again, she would not even look at her, let alone speak to her. Such was her hatred for the woman who had condemned her to a miserable life empty of a mother's love. But today, Jess stared at her coolly and felt nothing.

"Daughter, I'm so glad to see you," her mother stepped forward, opening her arms for hug.

Jess dodged the embrace. "Has something happened?"

"No, I just wanted to see you. I've missed you. I saw your story on TV and found you."

"I see. Would you like some tea?"

"I won't say no."

Entering the house, Jess's mother looked around and said, "Wow, they said that you have a factory and everything, but I wouldn't have guessed it from this house."

"This is my grandmother's house."

"Oh. Are these your children?"

"Berta, go upstairs, please."

Once Jess and her mother were alone, she poured the tea and sat down opposite the older woman, waiting for the question that was bound to follow. Her mother took her time and prattled about nonsense that Jess had no interest in.

"Have you found Esme and Bella?"

"No, unfortunately. I know that they went to good families and changed their names."

"That's wonderful!"

Jess curled her lip but said nothing. "Why did you come here?"

"I told you, to see you."

"I'll ask you one more time. Why did you come here?" Jess stared at her mother coldly, and when the woman saw that there was no sense in beating around the bush, she finally got to the point.

"I'm having some trouble as I owe money to a few serious people. I'm in a difficult situation."

"Right. So you came to ask for money?"

"Not only that, I wanted to see you too."

"You came to ask for money. I won't give you a cent. I can see that you're still using."

"I'm not, I swear!"

"Your hands are shaking! I'm not giving you any money. I can help you get treatment at a rehabilitation centre, and then find you a job. That's it."

Her mother's face changed in an instant, plunging Jess into the past. "I don't need rehab! I don't have a problem. If I'd known you were this greedy, I'd never have come here," the woman said and stood up.

"I'm not greedy, I simply don't want to fund your death. I'm willing to get you treatment, despite our past."

"You can get yourself treatment. Give me the money, I really need it."

Jess glared at her and said, "Who do you owe?"

"People in the area."

"Write down the address. I'll go there myself tomorrow, but you have to promise me something."

"Of course, what?"

"Don't ever come here again. Don't ever talk to me again. You and I are strangers. It's true. I used to think that people change, but seeing you, I realize that they don't. Now leave."

While her mother wrote down the address, Jess scooped up whatever groceries she had in the refrigerator and handed the bag to her mother, before closing the door behind her.

Her mother's arrival really affected Jess, even though she had stayed strong throughout the encounter. Jess cried all day, unable to understand the reason for her sadness. The reason was simple: she was again confronted with the fact that no one had ever needed her except her children. But she had to be strong for her children, while she wanted to be small and weak too.

Jess thought she could never be surprised again, but other people kept proving her wrong. The stab in the back came from her best friend and business partner. Through all these years of working with Taylor, Jess remembered how much she had helped her and remained incredibly grateful. She spared no money on gifts and divided the profits equally, even though Taylor had been neglecting her duties for a while. Jess first saw Taylor's other side was when she learned about a big deal that had been struck behind her back. The money disappeared—into Taylor's pocket, as it later turned out. Jess did not want to bring the situation to a head and, in an attempt to resolve the issue peacefully, came to her friend's house.

"Taylor, we've worked side by side for many years and I've

always appreciated what you do, but I recently discovered something unpleasant."

"Hm, what was it?" Taylor was all ears, and if Jess did not already know the truth, she would not have doubted Taylor's innocence.

"Someone sold the manufacturing rights for our products to China."

"No way! There must be a mistake."

"I know it was you. We've conducted an investigation and uncovered documents and transactions. We've suspended the deal because it's illegal."

"Well, that was quick." Taylor replied without a trace of embarrassment.

"I don't understand why you did this. Don't you have enough money?"

"No, I don't."

"Why go behind my back? You know our journey from beginning to end. You remember how we started out."

"I do, and I know that if it wasn't for me, you wouldn't have anything. I'm sick of being the friend at your beck and call. You owe everything you have to me!"

"Yes, I've said so more than once, yet you forget that the work was mine. I was the one who didn't sleep at night, sewing for days on end to keep up with the orders."

"Well done! I did a lot too, yet I only get the scraps."

"But you barely work these days. Others do everything for you."

"Jess, we can argue about this endlessly. I should get what I'm owed, and I think we should split the company in half. We started it together, after all."

"You're already getting almost as much as I am."

"Yet it's your name on all the billboards."

Jess stared at Taylor and couldn't believe the words coming out of her mouth. They say money ruins people. Not true. Money simply exposes people for who they are, and speeds up the process of corruption. Money also gives rise to a terrible sin–pride–which destroy not only people, but entire worlds.

"Do you realize that you're destroying our friendship right now?"

"There never was a friendship. Just business."

"There was, you just forgot. I'll always remember the young woman who came to buy gifts for her nephews. You were different back then."

"Oh, whatever. Let's resolve this fairly and we can go our separate ways, since I revolt you so much."

"Fairly? Everything was fair, but you went against the company! No one gave you permission to sell the rights. There are documents that will have to be made public. You should resign, otherwise you'll be faced with irreversible consequences, which I'd rather avoid."

"We'll see about that," Taylor sneered. "It's time for you to go."

Jess did not go home, but decided to remain in the office and review all of Taylor's paperwork. Although Jess ran the business honestly and paid all salaries and taxes, something in Taylor's words frightened her. She considered what her friend might have planned and invited Allan to the office the next morning. As soon as he arrived, Jess told him the whole story from beginning to end.

"She wants half the company? But there are no grounds."

"That's why I asked you to come. She sounded so sure that I thought, what if she's been preparing some documents for a long time? Or maybe I signed something once? I don't know."

"No, that won't happen. Look, it's going to be fine. There's only one thing you can do now, and that's to report her for fraud."

"I don't want to take that step. She has a family."

"Jess, that's not how you run a business. It's either you or her. Do you understand?"

"Yes, but let's wait. I feel better now that I've told you everything," Jess smiled sadly.

Allan had no choice but to agree with her. He could not put pressure on his client, especially at a time like this. He hugged her goodbye and, promising that it would all sort itself out, left.

A month after talking to Taylor, Jessica received a letter from court. The letter did not explain what the summons related to. Allan learned more about the case a little later. It turned out that Taylor had taken all the important documents and was claiming full rights to the company. Jess could not believe that her ex-friend could lie so blatantly. And for what? Was money worth losing one's last shred of decency?

There were gruelling court hearings, after which Jessica staggered home in utter exhaustion. She fought for the truth, but it appeared that no one believed her, despite all the evidence she provided. Taylor's name was listed on many of the documents, and she claimed that Jess was nothing more than a figurehead, while Taylor actually ran the company. Taylor insisted that she was the one who came up with the toy design and created the drawings. After six months in court, Jess had no strength left to fight.

One day, as she rocked in a chair by the window, she heard, "Mom, what's going on?"

It was the first time Berta had ever called her 'Mom'. Jessica turned to the child, and her eyes filled with tears. "Come here, baby."

Hugging the growing girl and feeling her warmth, Jess made a decision that she thought she should have made earlier.

"You smell so good. Like chocolates."

"Are you okay?"

"Don't worry about it. Just some issues at work."

"What happened?"

"It's too hard to explain."

"Well, explain using simple words."

"I'm going to have to give Heart Flame away."

"Why?"

"Because Auntie Taylor wants it for herself."

"But aren't you in charge there?"

"I am."

"So why should you give it to her?"

"It's a complicated situation."

The girl pulled away and thought for a minute. "When I came to the children's home, I was wearing a beautiful sweater with blue flowers embroidered by my mother. The carers wanted to take it away, but I cried so much that they took pity on me. Then I met Irma. She was the oldest in our group. Irma was so aggressive that everyone was afraid of her. She liked the sweater as much as I did. She made fun of me at first, then she hit me, but I refused to give her the sweater. Later, Irma cut it to shreds with scissors, but I kept the flowers, together with my other valuables."

Pain pierced Jess's heart. She held the girl's hands and, gazing into her eyes, whispered, "I'll do everything in my power so that no one ever hurts you again."

"I know. But now you must do everything in your power so that they don't hurt you."

Jess thought about Roberta's words for a long time. Such simple words, yet they had struck a chord. Why were people bullying her? Although Jess could not protect herself in the past, she could today. Yes, if she honestly and fairly believed that Taylor had more rights to the company, she would have given it away at once. But the situation was unfair and that was the point! Jess was the one who taught the workers how to sew, Jess was the one who spent nights at the factory, checking product quality, and Jess was the one who attended the presentations and negotiations.

"I will defend myself!" She told herself confidently.

Allan came to her house before the next court hearing.

"What's the matter? Why are you here? The court is in an hour."

"I wanted to tell you that everything will be fine. I know things are difficult and you're tired of all this, but hold on, okay? I've brought you something. A trifle."

Reaching into his coat pocket, Allan pulled out something small and nondescript. It was a necklace of edible beads and the words "Good Luck" written on it. Jess smiled as she accepted the gift.

"I saw it in the store and decided to buy it. I can't really give you presents, since we still have a business relationship," Allan was clearly embarrassed.

"Thank you, my dear friend. Thank you for supporting me and being there for me. I'll never forget your kindness."

"All right, I'll see you in court. Stay strong. You look great, by the way!" He shouted as he ran down the steps.

Jess couldn't help feeling anxious. Of course, she was ready for any outcome, having convinced herself that even if she lost the case, it would not be the end of the world. The most important thing was that everyone was alive and well. Of course, it would impact the workers and she was not sure how she would look after them, but she would come up with something.

Jess drove up to the courthouse and sat in the car for a long time. She startled when her phone rang. It was Allan.

"Jess! Where are you?" He sounded agitated.

"In the parking lot, I'll be right there."

"Taylor has agreed to a settlement. She's willing to be bought out and ready to sign whatever is needed!"

"My God!" Jess could not believe it.

"I know!"

"What made her do it? Are you sure this isn't another trick?"

"I'm sure! She realized that she's facing time for fraud. She's ready to accept compensation and step away from the business."

"How much is she asking for?"

"It's a significant amount, but you come out on top in any case."

"Got it. I'm coming."

***

A gentle summer breeze blew in through the slightly open window, stirring the white tulle. The children tumbled around the yard, bursting into happy laughter. Watching them, tenderness blossomed in Jess's heart, spreading throughout her body. Despite the hardships, betrayals, misfortunes, losses, physical pain, and mental anguish, she had still found happiness. She was loved and she loved in turn. Many things could have put out the fire in her soul, but it kept burning bright and eventually led her to success. Everything she had, she had achieved with her own two hands. She knew that another disaster could arrive on her doorstep tomorrow, but she also knew that Jessica Meadow could deal with it.

2

Hate

Hate
A Novel

Kira met Kim at an exhibition. He was an intelligent and well-read boy from a wealthy family. She was a long-awaited child, spoiled and used to the world revolving around her. Kim fell in love with Kira at first sight. A petite girl with hair as smooth as silk, she looked so fragile that Kim could not imagine the strength hidden within this delicate flower.

Kira was only 18 when she got married. They graduated from university together and grew as a couple. Kim had been born with a silver spoon in his mouth and had no idea about the adult world, the world of careers and money. Somehow, Kira knew about it all. She was embarrassed to live off her husband's parents, so she came up with one business idea after another. It was worth noting that each one was successful, and all Kim needed to do was follow his wife's directions. Kira was the grey cardinal in their relationship, but she preferred it this way. She did not seek the throne, leaving it for her husband.

In the morning, she would put make-up on her drab features, gradually transforming into a completely different person. Kim did not like Kira wearing make-up. He preferred her natural beauty, which did not exist, but he thought she looked simply angelic.

"I've struck a deal with the new suppliers. The contract has been drawn up, so I'm just waiting for you to confirm."

"Who are they?" Kim asked.

"Our trusty partners," Kira smiled. "They have a factory and produce high-quality building materials. It's a good deal for us; we'll be able to triple our turnover."

"I see. I'll sign it by lunch today."

"No, I need it by 10."

"Whatever you say, baby doll. Well, I'm off. See you at work?"

"Of course."

Kira's face lit up as she stepped outside. The snow was falling in large flakes. What a wonderful, magical time of the year. She was not surprised at all to see her car covered in snow. Kim never cleaned it for some reason. She supposed that he was used to other people taking care of him ever since he was a child. This was the problem with an only child – they grew up very egocentric.

"Three meetings today. How am I going to get everything done by lunch?" Kira said to herself as she drove along the snow-covered roads. "If you get them to knock down the price, you can recoup the investments and start turning a profit in 5 years. Then some quick renovations and finding tenants for the vacant premises. I wonder how much space we'll occupy. Remember to meet with the designer!"

Kira parked her car beside a large, abandoned building, touched up her makeup, and got out. A crowd of men met her at the entrance.

"Good morning, Kira," the owner's lawyer greeted her.

"Good morning, Michael and everyone else here!"

"Are you alone?" the lawyer asked in surprise.

"Yes, why?"

"Oh, it's nothing. We just expected you to bring an adviser with you."

"You underestimate me," Kira said sweetly. "Shall we go inside? We can check everything again and have a look at the paperwork. Have you read the contract I sent you yesterday?"

"Yes, and I must say that we strongly disagree with some of the points."

"I think I can provide you with sufficient evidence to support my proposal."

"Let the negotiations begin!" Michael exclaimed, opening the door for Kira.

The building was indeed in a deplorable state, as Kira had noted the first time, but she could envisage how it would look once she cleaned it all up. The important thing was the land, and it was worth fighting for. A good area, not too far from the centre, plus the high traffic. Kira knew this, so the owners were bound to know this too.

"Michael," Kira began, "repairing this building will cost many times more than its current price. I don't want to waste anyone's time, so I'll be straight with you. I know that you're probably unsatisfied with the price we've offered, but the commercial property market is quite flat at the moment and, as any financial analyst will tell you, it'll be more profitable for you to agree to our offer and invest the funds into something liquid and profitable. Make the money work for you, so to speak."

"But you must know that we're selling the land, not the building. You can demolish the building and build a new one."

"Building it will take several years!" Kira threw up her hands. "When are we supposed to start working? That's not your concern, of course," she added softly. "We're offering you a deal not because we're trying to be clever, but because this is the real situation on the market. It'll take time to find a new buyer and negotiating a price with them will take even longer. You'll suffer a loss in any case. I won't pressure on you since the decision is yours. My only request is – could you give us an answer before the end of the week so that we know to keep looking?"

The experienced lawyer looked at this fragile woman and secretly admired her ability to negotiate. He knew the truth of her words.

"Understood, Kira. We'll let you know."

"Thank you for the meeting, Michael. It was lovely to see you again."

Kira called Kim from the car.

"Well, did they say yes?"

"No, but I think they will. They don't have any buyers. Besides, I didn't drop the price by much."

"Well, you know best."

"I'm going to see the designer now, he has prepared a plan and calculations, so I won't be in the office until three."

"Isn't it too early for these meetings? You haven't even got a deal yet."

"Trust me, I do everything at the right time."

Kira often noticed that her husband tried to put the brakes on her endeavours. It was frustrating, of course, but, on the whole, she would never trade him for someone else. Kira felt happy with him from the very first day. All those years ago, she had immediately felt like they had met in a previous life and were thus destined to be together in this life. They were in no hurry to have children. Kira wanted a career and to mingle in society, although Kim occasionally pestered her about having a baby.

A stack of papers for signing and a heap of other tasks were waiting for her at the office.

"I've only been gone half a day," Kira said in surprise.

"We've been sent the price lists and contracts. The previous supplier has also issued his invoices."

"Alright, I'll take a look. I'm not going to make it home tonight, am I?" Kira smiled.

"Goodness, no, Mrs. Blanchett! You'll get it all done in no time!" exclaimed her faithful assistant.

Sitting at the dressing table in the evening and washing off her make-up, Kira replayed the day and all its victories in her head. She occasionally had bad days, but this never upset her. She knew that a new day would arrive when she would achieve everything she wanted. She was a fighter by nature.

Kim bought Kira an island holiday for their 10th wedding anniversary. Kira had no desire to go because she kept feeling unwell lately, but she pretended to be overjoyed for her husband's sake. Kim rarely organised anything himself and tended to give her money on special occasions, so Kira really appreciated this gesture.

The couple had travelled to many countries over their years of marriage. They usually kept busy with trips to museums and exhibitions while on holiday, so Kira could not imagine what she would do on a small island. The flight went well except that Kira felt nauseated. Fortunately, it settled upon arrival, and Kira felt a growing happiness when they boarded the boat waiting for them. As they slid over the glittering azure waves, Kim took his wife's hand. The past ten years felt like a mirage, and they were as in love with each other as before.

The island turned out to be very sweet. It only had one hotel, hidden behind the lush and exuberant greenery. Kira liked the solitude, and she could finally take a break from the cold days filled with work. They had agreed not to talk about the business while on holiday. Kira continued to experience nausea in the mornings, and one day, Kim obtained a pregnancy test to check his theory.

"I'm afraid," Kira said. "What if it's positive?"

"What do you mean? It'll be a blessing!"

"What about work? What about my project? I must finish it and launch it!"

"Kira, the job will still be there. Plus, we already have so many of these buildings that delaying one of them won't make a difference."

"Oh, bother! On the other hand, it's not the worst time.

We're standing on our own two feet, and Mum's been going on and on about it."

"Hush. Is it ready yet?" Kim interrupted impatiently.

Kira glanced at the test, but it showed only one line. "It's negative," she exhaled.

"Are you sure?" Kim didn't believe her and snatched the test out of her hand. "Yes, just one line. Well then, we need to find a different cause for your illness."

"I'll have a blood test. I'll go to the doctor as soon as we're back."

Kira considered her emotions on the way to breakfast. On the one hand, she was glad that they were not having a baby, because it meant that everything would continue as before, but on the other hand, she felt a bit upset.

They splashed around in the gentle sea after breakfast. Kim swung her through the waves. Kira was light anyway and seemed to weigh nothing at all in the water. Life was worth living for such moments, when there was only him, her, the sky and the sea.

Rinsing the remaining sand off her body, Kira jumped when Kim abruptly screamed. "Kim! What is it?" she yelled.

"Kira," Kim ran into the bathroom, "it's positive!"

"My God, you scared me. It's positive?"

"Yes, yes!" Kim was ecstatic. Kira had not seen her husband so happy about something in a long time. He came up to her, kissed her and whispered, "Congratulations, you're going to be a mum!"

Kira smiled.

They spent the next day discussing how to restructure their business so that their life's work would continue while

Kira was on maternity leave. They came up with an excellent plan.

On their return home, everyone noticed Kira's dramatic transformation. Her eyes shone, and her face was sun-kissed and joyful.

The first trimester was especially difficult. Kira felt constantly sleepy and found it hard to focus. All this had a negative impact on the business, so they had to hire a new employee. A young woman with the mysterious name of Asia seemed very responsible and her good looks were a bonus. She was the exact opposite of Kira, a tall and curvy brunette who radiated energy and strength. However, Kira was taken aback by her forcefulness since she herself was a more subtle negotiator.

"Asia," Kira said once. "I like your work, but the way you talk to clients is unacceptable at times. You need to tone it down. They're businesspeople, after all, and not used to such behaviour."

Asia only laughed. "Oh, Kira, I've spoken to all sorts of people, and believe me, the way I talk to them is exactly what they need."

"Nevertheless, I'd like you to stick to my policy. I use a different approach in my work."

"Whatever you say. You're the boss."

Something in this wild woman made Kira uncomfortable, but she had no choice but to work with her. Asia grasped everything on the fly, and there was simply no time to look for a replacement. The deadlines could not wait. It was unfortunate that Kim was not as good at negotiations, and he had been barred from ever trying again after he let a supplier slip the hook last time.

Kira felt better once she was in her second trimester, and immediately took back the reins of management. Asia was sent to another department.

"Are you sure you weren't too quick to send her away?" Kim asked. "You'll need her help again when you're on maternity leave."

"No, honey, she worries me. She's too wild and hard to control. I told her how she should behave, but she just listened and did it her own way. I'll find a replacement while I still have time."

Kira continued to tirelessly build the family business. Every week, she held a briefing with her husband and rejoiced at the growing profits. They lived very well, with all the comforts, fancy clothes and other attributes. The only thing that changed was the house. They bought a larger one with a cosy garden, perfect for children. Kira immediately called in some labourers so that an adorable playground with swings stood in the garden a week later.

Kira gave birth in the best hospital in the city. The birth was difficult due to her fragile constitution. Kira was barely alive when the baby was placed on her stomach, and even forgot to ask its gender. Once Kira regained her senses, she asked the nurse, "Is it a boy?"

"A girl. You have a healthy little girl, Mrs. Blanchett. She's adorable, you know."

"Thank you," Kira replied and slipped back into oblivion. When she opened her eyes, she saw Kim holding a small bundle in his arms.

"How are you, my love? The doctors said not everything went according to plan. You should have taken me with you."

"No, Kim. It was awful enough as it is. If you were there too, I wouldn't have had the strength for both of us. You panic at the sight of blood."

"Do you want to hold her?"

"Not right now."

"Do you want to go back to sleep? Don't worry, I'll stay here."

Kira smiled. She was no longer worried about anything, for she believed that the hardest part was over.

When she felt a little stronger, she slipped out of bed and approached the cot. "Gosh," Kira uttered in surprise. "She's the spitting image of me. My little girl, my daughter. Did I really create you? There's no greater miracle in the world than the birth of a child! How does one tiny piece make a whole baby?"

Kira touched the baby gently, stroked the pale hair and held her hand. She smelled indescribable, delicate and sweet. Love pierced Kira's heart. She had thought that she loved Kim, but as she gazed at her daughter, she understood that she had known nothing about love until now.

Kira's mother came to help with the child. She was a gentle and caring woman, who did not get in anyone's way. Naturally, Kira was against her mother taking care of her granddaughter, given that she had already raised her own children, but her mother insisted. It was definitely easier with a caring grandmother around. She could calm the baby down in a couple of seconds, as if by magic.

"Kira dear, why haven't you picked a name yet? It's been long enough."

"Kim wants to name her after his grandmother but I'm against it. I gave birth to her, so I should be the one to name her."

"And which name did you come up with?"

"Olivia," Kira smiled. "That's what I called her when she was still in my stomach."

"It's lovely. Which name did Kim suggest?"

"Sarah."

"Why don't you make it her middle name?"

"He doesn't want it as the middle name. Well, we'll see how it turns out."

Olivia was a calm child, to her mother's delight. She slept peacefully through the night, only waking up at around 4 a.m. to feed. When Kira was pregnant, she thought that being stuck at home on maternity leave would be unbearable, but now, she could not understand why she would want to leave this bundle of joy for someone else. Of course, this was less convenient for Kim, since his workload had increased in his wife's absence, and he often had to stay back late. This did not worry Kira.

Once the girl was three months old, her parents officially named her Olivia. The name suited her very well, and Kim grew to love it too.

"My darling girl, my princess," he would whisper in her ear. "Daddy will do anything for you, anything. You will have anything you want."

"Tone it down," Kira urged him. "God forbid she grows up spoiled."

"She won't," Kim insisted. "I won't give you to anyone!"

The baby only grinned in response, not yet understanding her father's words.

When Olivia turned one, Kira finally decided to return to work. The girl was left with her grandmother.

Kira was unpleasantly surprised when she arrived at the office. Kim had changed the furniture and the layout, so that the workplace was now unrecognizable. The staff had also changed. Instead of the excellent, kind and comfortable people she had previously worked with, strangers walked robot-like around the office. Kim had not said a word to her about these changes. Kira hurried to his office, which was still in the same place, and ran into Asia in the doorway.

"Hello, Mrs. Blanchett!" Asia greeted her.

"Hello. What are you doing here? Don't you work on the 4th floor?"

"Oh, I transferred to your husband's department a year ago."

"I see," Kira replied, trying to keep her face perfectly blank. "Well, I wish you every success in your new position."

Kim was on the phone when Kira came in. He winked at her cheerfully and pointed to a chair. Having quickly fended off the annoying caller, Kim turned and beamed at his wife.

"I'm so glad to see you, dear. I thought that you might not make it to the office and return home."

"You know that I'm not one to change my plans. I see you've altered everything in here."

"Yes, I forgot to tell you. Do you like it?"

"It's less cosy in my opinion."

"Yes, I said the same thing to Asia, but she insisted that fashion has changed, and this is how it's done now."

"So, she did this?" Kira felt herself getting angry.

Kim walked up and chuckled as he gave his wife a hug. "You're so cute when you're angry. You pull such a funny face, just like Olivia! Don't be mad. We'd have had to renovate sooner or later."

"I didn't see Miss Sawyer, Tom or Andy..."

"Yes, I had to let them go," Kim pulled a face. "They weren't keeping up with their new responsibilities."

"Is my office still there at least?" Kira deflated like a balloon.

"Of course. We didn't touch anything in there. I know how much you hate it when someone touches your things without asking."

"Well, that's one piece of good news. Okay, I'll go and settle in to my new/old place."

Kira spent the day trying to wrap her head around the company's new business. She felt like a fish out of water. Kira pushed down her anger and tried to get used to her new surroundings, but it did not work. She also noticed that Asia had begun to act very much like the CEO in her absence.

'Fine,' Kira thought, 'I'll keep my thoughts to myself for today.'

She returned home feeling dejected. The only bright spot was her nearest and dearest waiting for her in the warmth and comfort of her house.

"How did it go?" Her mother asked as she ladled out a fragrant soup.

"It's hard to tell. Kim changed everything in there, or rather, that nasty girl did. I'd disliked her from the start."

"Who is she?"

"A business shark!"

"Asia, if I remember correctly?" Mom smiled.

"That's the one. Half the employees are new; I don't know them at all. And they've changed all the work software. I spent half the day just reading the instructions!"

"Tomorrow is a new day, my darling. Things will work out. You'll understand the software and get used to the new colleagues. You'll put your stamp on the business."

"Thank you, Mum," Kira replied affectionately. "It's so nice to be home."

Kira's heart lifted after a filling dinner. She ought to listen to her mother, because tomorrow really was a new day.

The next morning, she was up bright and early, and ready for the new working day by the time her husband woke up.

"I'd like you not to stay back at work anymore," she instructed Kim.

"Why? Are we expecting something?" Kim grew tense.

"No, we're not expecting anything. I'm back at work now, so there's no need for you stay back. I want us to spend our evenings together as a family again."

"I'll certainly try."

The second day at work went better than the first. Kira rearranged the furniture to give the office a makeover, although it still looked worse than before.

Nor did Kira remain silent when Asia verbally attacked one of the employees again. Leaving her office, Kira approached the young woman and asked firmly, "What's going on here?"

"It's nothing, just some issues regarding the new project," Asia replied calmly.

"Asia," Kira began, raising her voice a little so that everyone could hear her, "I want you to remember where you are! This isn't some massage parlour you've worked at before. I ask that you follow the well-defined rules and speak to your subordinates in a respectful tone."

Asia's face twisted. Yes, Kira knew exactly where to strike. Not only had this upstart wormed her way onto Kira's floor and changed absolutely everything, she also dared to spoil the atmosphere with her rudeness! No, Kira would not stand for it.

"Do I make myself clear?" Kira drove the point home.

"Crystal clear, Mrs. Blanchett."

Kira had forgotten about the conflict with Asia until Kim brought it up that evening. "What happened with Asia today?"

Kira raised her eyebrows. "How do you know about that? Did she complain about it to you?"

"No, she just mentioned it."

"Kim, I don't see why a company owner should care about such trifles, but I'll tell you since you're asking. I've noticed that Asia is creating a tense working atmosphere. In my opinion, such shouting and fighting are unacceptable in our company, and it was my job to put her back in her place. That's all."

"Okay, honey. You know best."

"When did she tell you this? Wasn't she in a meeting all day?" Kira asked suspiciously.

"I met her in the smoke room," Kim replied without hesitation.

"All right then," Kira calmed down. She trusted her husband implicitly because he was a decent man. Besides, he loved her with all his heart.

For the next five months, Kira tried to adapt to the new team and new ways of doing things but alas, she could not. Her clients had gone to Asia, and Kira no longer had a place in the office. The decision to find another job did not come lightly. After all, Kira had put a lot of effort into establishing this company. They were her ideas, her work, her plans. It was hard to part with what she had built over the years.

"Have you really thought it through?" Kim asked for days on end.

"Yes, I've weighed up all the pros and cons. Things are going well, and you don't need me here anymore. I'll find something new."

Kim did not insist. Kira found what she was looking for and joined a small company that had not yet made a name for itself, with a small but exceptionally friendly and tight-knit team. Kira was welcomed with open arms and gained their love and respect as soon as they saw her in action. Her job was to obtain permits from the relevant organizations for construction, redevelopment, landscaping, and so on. It required a lot of talking and travelling, but Kira managed.

Time was not kind to Kim as the years passed. He did not move much but ate a lot. Meanwhile, Kira had not changed a bit. Of course, there were tiny wrinkles here and there, but she looked much younger than her age.

The 20th anniversary of their life together was approaching.

Kira could not believe that so many years had passed. The feelings were not as intense as before, they had transformed into something other, but Kim and Kira remained each other's dearest and closest person.

Kira kept working at the same company and did not grow bored of her job. Plus, she had found new friends in the office opposite. Every lunch time, they shared cheerful stories about their work. She could also buy wonderful holiday packages from them at ridiculous prices.

"I finally decided where I'd like to go!" Kira exclaimed as she ran into Isla's office.

"I thought you'd never go anywhere," her friend said with a grin. "Take a seat. Let's have a look. When and where?"

"Well, Kim will be back from Japan on the 23rd, and he'll need a couple of days to recover and sort out a few work matters, so I think the 27th would be ideal. I'm looking at 5-7 days, no more than that."

"You still haven't said where."

"How about the Caribbean?"

"Sure, there's a good hotel, but it doesn't have any discounts. I can give you 10% off. Would that work?"

"Yep. I've brought photocopies of our documents. Can you fill it out yourself?"

"Of course," Isla replied.

When Kira handed her the photocopies, Isla froze, her mouth slightly open.

"What is it?" Kira asked worriedly.

"Um, it's nothing," Isla pulled herself together. "Is that your husband?"

"Yes, why?"

"His face looks familiar."

"Oh! You might have seen him in a magazine."

"I guess."

Kira gave it no more thought and returned to work. She forgot about the strange incident at the travel agency until a couple of days later, when Isla appeared at her workplace.

"Can we talk in private somewhere?"

"Has something happened?"

"Let's go outside."

Throwing on her coat, Kira hurried out the door after her friend. Isla took a long time getting comfortable on a bench, then spent a while lighting her cigarette. Kira grew anxious.

"Listen," Isla finally said, "I've been wondering whether to tell you or not for several days, but I've decided that you should know the truth. Look, this is a list of trips booked through our agency." Isla handed Kira a list. "A young woman named Asia Spencer always came to fill out the paperwork, and she always listed the same companion – Kim Blanchett. I didn't know he was your husband until I saw the documents you'd brought."

Kira held the list in her hand and could not believe what she was hearing. Her cheeks were aflame. "They go on business trips," she whispered.

"No," Isla brushed away the suggestion. "Many of them were romantic trips, she said so herself."

"Why are you telling me this?" Kira asked with tears in her eyes.

"I'm your friend, you should know the truth."

"Have you considered the possibility that I don't want to know about this? That this discovery will destroy my family?"

Isla was silent. Kira left, clutching the hateful piece of paper. She asked to leave work early and went home. She allowed herself to burst into tears only once she was parked in front of the house. Kira sat like this for an hour and then started wondering. 'When did it start? Five years ago? Ten years ago? It probably happened when I was pregnant with Olivia and that viper moved to our floor. But I didn't notice anything. Everything was fine. Could the whole thing be a lie? Maybe they're just business trips? It can't be true! Right, I'll ask Kim tonight. There has to be a reasonable explanation." Kira tried to calm her brain down, but her heart knew the truth.

Her face when she entered the house alarmed her mother.

"What's wrong, darling?" Mum asked.

"Nothing," Kira waved her away. "I don't feel very well. I'm going to have a lie down."

"Would you like some soup?"

"No, thanks. I don't want anything."

Kira went into the bedroom but could not stay still. Evening was still hours and hours away and she could not endure the wait until Kim came home. Taking out her mobile, Kira dialled her husband's number. He kept hanging up, but she kept calling.

"Kira, I'm in a meeting," he said, finally picking up the phone. "What's the matter?"

"You have to come home right away," Kira told him coldly.

"My God, has something happened? Is Olivia all right?"

"Come home now."

Kira hung up and waited. Kim arrived quickly. Running into the bedroom and seeing the streaks of mascara on his wife's face, he realized that something truly terrible had happened. Kira rarely cried.

"What's wrong?" he exclaimed.

Handing Kim the printout from the travel agency, Kira asked, "Is this true? Are you having an affair?"

Kim glanced at the papers and said nothing. Silence could only mean one thing in this situation.

"So, it is true?" she asked, still holding on to a sliver of hope.

"Yes." Kim met his wife's eyes, and she knew that he was telling the truth.

Kira turned to the window, feeling like a powerful sledgehammer had smashed her over the head.

"Did it start when I was pregnant?" Kira asked, sounding unlike herself.

"Yes."

"So all these years..."

"Kira, I'd never leave this family. It's not serious."

"Not serious?" Kira shouted, turning to face him. "Is breaking my heart into pieces not serious? Is betraying my soul not serious? You meant everything to me. We shared every joy and tribulation. How could you? How could you?" She burst into tears again, covering her small and miserable face.

"Kira, please. I'll fire her today. Please forgive me."

He came closer, but she grew hysterical and kept repeating, "Go away, go away, go away."

After Kim left, Kira lay on the floor for a long time, unable to get up. She could hear Olivia's voice downstairs, so it was about 4 p.m. Kira needed to stand up and wash her face so as not to frighten her daughter, but she could not. There was a soft knock at the door and her mother came in.

"Kira, are you all right?" she asked, opening the door carefully. "My God, why are you on the floor? Is something hurting?"

"My soul," Kira replied inaudibly.

"Kira, darling, please get up. Won't you tell me what happened?"

"Kim's been cheating on me for the past ten years. Ten long years of lies and betrayal."

Her mother stood dumbstruck.

"Leave me be, Mum. I want to be alone."

Kira continued to lie on the floor, curled into a ball. Strangely, she felt nothing at all. There was an emptiness inside her, like a scorched field. Kira stood up, glanced at her face in the gathering dusk and was horrified. Her face was completely devoid of colour. Kira took a warm shower, put on a fluffy robe and went downstairs. The house was silent, but a light was on in the kitchen. Olivia and her mother were reading a book and drinking milk.

"Mummy!" Olivia cried and ran up to Kira. "Grandma said you were sick."

"No, baby. It's nothing. How was your day? Did anything interesting happen?"

"It was fine, but Miley was being mean again. She talked the other girls into excluding me from their games."

"What a rotten girl!"

"Yeah. But I didn't get upset and came up with my own game, and even the boys joined in."

"Well done! You're a clever little cookie. Are you reading already? What time is it?"

"It's almost nine," Her mother replied. "Time for bed."

"Mummy, will you sing me a song?"

"Of course, let's go."

Kira completed the evening ritual, then went back downstairs to her mother. She had to calm her down too.

"How are you feeling?" Mum asked.

"I don't know," Kira sighed. "Don't worry about me, okay?"

"What are you going to do?"

"I've got such a headache..."

"I'll get you a pill. Try to sleep."

And Kira did fall asleep.

It all seemed like a dream in the morning. At first, Kira could not bring herself to face reality. An unbearable pain pierced her heart when she remembered what had happened. Her thoughts were jumbled, while her imagination threw up images.

"So, you've been leading a double life all these years," she whispered, "You've been cheating on me even when I was pregnant with your child, whom you'd wanted for years. How is this possible? Why did you do this to me?"

Kira could not process that this had happened to her. She tried to be a decent person and be good to other people. Kira had never done anything nasty, and she always thought that such punishments were sent for bad deeds. How was this possible? Kim's betrayal made it difficult to breathe. Sitting up in bed, she tried to suck in a mouthful of air. A little longer and she thought she might die. Kira rushed to the window and threw it open, hoping that the fresh air would save her. The frosty December air burned her cheeks.

"It's almost New Year," Kira uttered and burst into tears.

How to live? How to keep living with this knowledge? Yet she could not die either. Olivia was still young. She was at that tender preadolescent age, and Kira should be delighting in it, instead of dealing with all this.

Still in a daze, Kira took a shower and then rang work. She could not think clearly, hear what was being said to her or remember much of what was happening. It was as if she was living in the past, thinking back to the moment that serpent had shown up and stolen her husband. Although, if not this one, it might have been another. Perhaps it had nothing to do with the serpent? No, them too!

"Do we have any sedatives in the house?" Kira asked her mother dryly.

Mum gave her a wary look. "Yes. I'll get you one."

"Tell me where they are, and I'll get one myself."

"Stop it, Kira! You're scaring me. I'll get you one myself."

'Oh dear,' Kira thought, 'she thinks I'm going to do something to myself. I'd never! But what if...' She began to doubt herself.

The pills had little effect. They slowed down her nervous system, but her heart and soul felt as raw as before.

'Is it cheating?' She wondered. 'This wasn't some one-time fling. It's been going on for years. Years of lies. So, he spent time with her and then came home to me? He kissed me with those lips and kissed Olivia. Was it all a game? Why did he live with me then? But he enjoyed going on vacation with us and reading Olivia books before bed.'

Kim's face appeared out of nowhere.

"Kira, little one, it's me," he said just like he used to and took her hand. "I'm sorry, it won't happen again. I'll cut off all contact with her and things will go back to normal. All these years, I blamed myself for what was going on, but I didn't know how to end it. I wanted to break up with her for a long time, but she threatened to tell you everything, so I left things as they were. I know I've hurt you."

Kira wanted to say something, but her tongue would not move. She felt paralysed.

'Oh my God, what did Mom give me?' she panicked. 'What if I remain like this forever? Well, fine! At least Kim will be by my side.'

Waking up in the morning, she tried to move her arm. Her arm and whole body worked just like before. It was all a dream.

When Kira came down to breakfast, she saw her mother, who looked like she was in mourning.

"Good morning, darling. Did you speak to Kim?"

"When?" Kira said in surprise.

"He came home yesterday. He slept in Olivia's room."

Kira understood that it had not been a dream.

"What have you decided?" Her mother probed.

"Nothing. He said that he would stop seeing her. I can't really remember."

"You have to forgive."

"Forgive what?"

"Him. He's your husband and the father of your child."

Kira peered into her face and abruptly asked, "Has Dad ever cheated on you?"

"No."

"Then you've been luckier with your husband than I've been with mine," Kira snapped. "How can you give me advice about something you have no idea about?"

"I might have no idea, but I've lived longer than you have. I don't want you to suffer later."

"Oh, Mum," Kira sighed. "He was with her for 10 years! Can you imagine? Ten long years. It would have been bad enough if it had happened once, but this..."

"I understand."

"You don't understand anything," Kira cut her off. "How can you understand if you've never been in my situation? Just drop it."

Kira called her lawyer to prepare her divorce papers. She had never tolerated lies and she would not start now. The pain that had turned to hatred ate away at her insides. Lying in bed at night, Kira imagined tying Kim up, and then slowly and sadistically cutting off the body part he had apparently thought with when he climbed atop Asia.

The phone rang the next day. It was Kim. "Kira, are you filing for divorce?" he asked.

"Yes, I can't live like this."

Kim knew his wife and knew that it was useless to argue with her once she had made a decision. "All right. But I need to talk to my mum first."

"What does your mother have to do with this?" Kira was puzzled.

"Nothing, of course, but I thought we signed a contract before we got married."

"The contract covered your real estate before marriage. We

acquired a lot more during our marriage than you had before me!" Kira seethed.

"Yes, of course, but I still sent the documents to my mother. Do you want Olivia to stay with you?"

"Yes! You can come over whenever you want, but you should warn me in advance so I can leave."

"Why are you being like this?"

"What about you?" Kira suddenly burst into tears. "For what? I'd loved you all these years. I was so proud of our marriage, of you. I served you faithfully, trying to make your life better! Why did you do this to me? I didn't deserve it, I was a good wife!"

"I know. It just happened..."

"You've destroyed me! I don't know how to go on or how to live without you."

Yes, he knew that perfectly well. He had thought about it for years. But if his conscience bothered him at first, eventually, it fell silent, and he began to find excuses for his betrayal. He forgot about morality and decency.

A couple of days later, a letter arrived from another serpent, Kim's mother. It began like this,

Hello, dear Kira!

I have heard about what happened and it is a shame, of course. I hope you can maintain good and friendly relations for Olivia's sake.

I will now get to the point. Our lawyers found some inconsistencies when they reviewed the documents you sent. The document contradicts the prenuptial agreement you signed 20 years ago. Based on the agreement, and the law will agree, you only have at your disposal what you bought with your own savings, of which you had none. I am sorry to have to tell you this, but I am counting on your understanding.

With best wishes,

Jenny Blanchett

"Why, you bitch!" Kira swore, which she had never done before.

She printed out the pages and skimmed through the points marked in red. It turned out that Kim's mother had drawn up quite a cunning contract 20 years ago, and Kira had not noticed. What a fool!

With shaking hands, she dialled Kim's number. He did not answer right away.

"Kim!" Kira exclaimed. "Did you see what your mother sent me?"

"I did," he replied wearily.

"Kim, that's not fair! I was the one who built the business in the first place! All the negotiations I conducted, all the energy I spent on repairs. The apartments, the houses – I did all that!"

"Kira, I can't talk right now. I'm in a meeting."

"Kim, you can't do this," Kira said desperately.

"There's nothing I can do. We have to follow the law. Our house will remain with Olivia, plus the car and a monthly allowance. I'm not denying that."

"Not denying? Not denying? It's supposed to stay with us, but you're also supposed to give me what I've earned over the years!"

Kim hung up the phone before she had even finished.

Kira stood frozen at the window, clutching her phone and papers. She could not believe that the man she had once loved had not only betrayed her in the most despicable way but was also refusing to act honourably. Although, why would he be honourable if he had been lying and cheating for 10 years? How could she not have noticed this sneakiness, this ignobility in him? When did he become so? Perhaps he had always been like this?

"No, I won't let you get away with this!" Kira hissed, clenching her fists.

She dialled the number of a partner she used to work with. "Hello, Sebastian? It's Kira Blanchett."

There was a laugh.

"I have your number, my dear! How's life?"

"I'm fine, thanks. I hope you're well too. Listen, I remember that you had a lawyer in your team who practically did my head in before the deal."

"Yes, Rapiro. He doesn't work here anymore. What happened?"

"Do you still have his contact details? I'm in the midst of a divorce and I suspect that my lawyer can't pull it off. It's a complicated case."

"I see. I'm sorry to hear that. I'll text you his number."

"Thank you very much. You're a lifesaver."

"Listen, since you're a free woman now, maybe you'd consider my last offer again?"

"Oh no, perhaps later," Kira replied coquettishly.

Kira called Rapiro at lunchtime. He did not handle divorces, but he gave her the number of Lex Lando, the best lawyer in town for such cases. Kira sent him the documents and waited for a week, with hate the only thing that sustained her during this time. First she imagined Kim crawling back to beg her forgiveness, but she would regally reject his advances and he would leave in tears, his head bowed. Then she imagined winning the lawsuit and the money healing her wounded pride. He would pay with either suffering or money for what he had done to their lives!

Unfortunately for Kira, these dreams were no more than that. Kim did not run after her and certainly did not cry at her feet.

The divorce proceedings also seemed uncertain. Lex agreed to take the case but did not promise anything. The marriage contract had been drawn up in a clever way, and the remaining couple of loopholes could not guarantee a win. But Kira did not lose hope and remained adamant. She prepared for the battle by collecting additional documents confirming her direct involvement in her husband's business.

Olivia started visiting her father on the weekends and, without meaning to, brought back news that were unbearable to Kira. Not only did Kim not waste any time grieving, he also began to build a nice little life with his new squeeze. Asia had replaced Kira completely. After every weekend, Kira swallowed handfuls of pills so she would not feel anything. She could not work, as if she had lost all her past skills. Deals fell apart before her eyes and negotiations went badly. Kira's boss encouraged her to take some paid leave, but she resigned instead.

Lying awake at night, she wondered what her life would have been like if she had not found out the shocking truth. By now, she thought it would have been better if everything had remained as it was. Kim would have never left his family.

They would still be happy, shopping for groceries, riding their bicycles, and going to the park or cafe.

"I gave you up too easily," Kira said into the dark. "You must be so pleased! I should have been smarter and played a game against you. Why did I dump it all at once? Oh, if that were the case, you wouldn't be you, Kira. You know that the truth is better than a bitter lie! But better for whom? My life is over."

Then came the divorce proceedings. They left Kira drained physically and emotionally. She was overcome with rage. Her internal state began to affect her appearance, making her look 10 years older. She constantly felt unwell and only revenge got her out of bed every morning.

Although she had not seen or spoken to Kim for almost a year, she continued to have conversations with him. In her imagination, he was mostly silent, while Kira could not stop talking. There was so much she wanted to say! However, the crux of the conversation was always the same.

Kira's mother, seeing what was happening to her daughter, showed unexpected forcefulness and sent her daughter to a psychotherapist. She took Kira to him in person.

Kira did not know what to say in the first session and barely spoke for the entire hour. She did not want to air her dirty laundry in front of a stranger.

"I don't like him and I'm not coming back," Kira told her mother as she left the office.

"If you won't see this one, you'll see another one. It's been a year, so it's time to return to your normal life. You're still alive! Don't forget that you have a daughter and a mother."

Kira listened to her mother. She knew she had no right

to make them suffer too. Therefore, she would try to clamber out of the hole she had fallen into.

At the next session, she opened up to the psychotherapist and told him everything. It made her feel a little better. She saw him for a year, and they tried a variety of things: practices, meditations, imaginary friendly dialogues with her husband, words of forgiveness and goodbyes. She felt like she found peace in the therapist's office, but resentment and bitterness seized her again as soon as she stepped outside. Kira could not accept what had happened. She could not, even though she remembered that humility was one of the steps to salvation.

Kira had barely recovered from the last blow when she was hit by another one. A wild rage seized her upon learning that she had lost in all the courts. Neither the pills nor the fancy psychological techniques helped. In addition, Olivia came back once again from her dad's house and let slip that Kim was expecting a new baby. Kira went completely berserk. She tore and smashed anything she could get her hands on. Kira's mother, frightened by her daughter's behaviour, even took Olivia to stay with her sister. When she returned, she found Kira surrounded by candles, with shredded wedding photos scattered all around her.

"My darling," her mother whispered, sinking down next to her, "are you hungry? Shall we go and eat? Then you can drink your medicine and go to bed." Mum spoke to Kira as if she was three years old again.

Kira stared at her with blank yet crazy eyes. "I'm hexing him," she said. "See, I'm pricking his eyes out. Something is bound to happen to him."

"You can't do that, darling. Come on, get up. Don't scare your mum, please."

"You saw how much I did for him, didn't you? I gave him everything I had! My best years, my life. I worked so hard to ensure that we had everything. I made him a business owner, even though he wasn't close to being one. Why, Mummy? What have I done that God is punishing me like this? I must have sinned or offended someone! It couldn't have just happened for no reason!"

"He's not punishing you," Mom continued in her soft voice, "it's the Lord's will. It happened for a reason, but it's not your fault. It just happened this way. There is no reason for it. It'll get easier soon, you'll see. You need to be patient, get through it, and life will return to normal. It will all work out; you've just got take baby steps. Take Mummy's hand and we'll take the medicine and go to bed."

Somehow, the woman managed to get Kira to obey. She took a sedative, ate a few spoonfuls of soup, and went to bed. In the meantime, her mother tidied up the trashed room. The flickering candlelight made the shredded wallpaper look especially frightening, while Kim's gouged out eyes in the photos forced the woman to cross herself.

Kira was feverish in the night. She plunged further and further down into an abyss, and thought the path led straight to hell. Kira awoke in hospital.

"I was sleeping next to her and woke up because she was delirious. She was burning up." Her mother told the doctor.

"Was she taking any medications?"

"Yes, a sedative, but it had been prescribed by her doctor. It's quite mild and hasn't caused such a reaction before."

"I see. Will you stay here for a while? The blood test results will come back soon, and then we'll know what's happening to your daughter."

The doctors were not pleased with the results. Kira's tests showed worsening inflammation, but no one could say why at this stage, so more tests were required.

Kira's self-preservation finally kicked in and she forgot about Kim while in hospital. The only thing she wanted was to go home.

When Kira's mother came to see her the next day, the doctor intercepted the older woman. "We have identified the cause – your daughter has breast cancer."

"No!" Her mother burst out.

"It's not fatal, so please try to calm down. We will remove her left breast before there are any metastases and then prescribe a course of chemotherapy. We hope that your daughter can handle it."

"Does she know?"

"Yes. The sooner she undergoes surgery, the better the chance of recovery."

Kira's mother could not bring herself to enter the room. Gathering her courage, she finally opened the door. Kira was gazing out the window. Seeing her mother, she calmly announced, "I have cancer."

"I know," Mum replied and started to cry.

"Come on, Mum, don't cry!" Kira said in her old commanding tone. "I'm not dying, for God's sake. It should be fine. We have to stay strong."

Mum hugged her daughter and they sat together for a long time.

The operation was successful like the doctors had promised. As the anaesthesia wore off, Kira felt like a wounded bird. Not only her will to fly, but even her wings were broken. How could she not blame Kim?

"Now I'm just like an Amazon," she consoled her mother while barely holding back her own tears.

It was only when she was alone in her room that she gave vent to her feelings and allowed herself to mourn her miserable life. She felt sorry for herself, for Kim, for Olivia and for her mother. How could the lives of so many depend on one sneaky, thieving person? And a woman too. Kira should not have pitied Kim, of course, for he had made his choice. But it was only while the drugs were working.

Kira found the first dressing very difficult. It felt strange to see pink and swollen skin covered with a crust where her breast had been so recently. But Kira quickly got back into a fighting spirit when she heard the doctor's plan of action. This was not the end.

"Kira, you have an important journey ahead of you. You need to undergo chemotherapy to prevent the spread of metastases to other areas. You must keep to a strict schedule and remain positive. Try to avoid any stressful situations. Do we have a deal?"

"How will I tolerate the chemo?"

"It'll be hard. Some tolerate it better and others worse."

"What about my hair?"

"It's best if you shave it off, but don't worry, it'll grow back," the doctor smiled. He wanted to say something supportive to this tiny woman.

Kira met many wonderful people during her chemotherapy. The sight of some horrified her, and she struggled to hide the pity in her eye because sick people did not like it. The treatment hit her hard, but she continued to cling to life. She remembered the following year only in snatches: the hospital, examinations and feeling poorly. Life began to return to her when she finally heard the long-awaited phrase, "We've beaten it!"

Kira could not really believe it until she saw the gleam in the doctor's eyes.

"Moreover, you'll be able to get a breast implant in a year's time. No one will be able to tell that you've had surgery."

Kira was over the moon. Could she finally return to her old life? She promised herself and God that she would never stoop to cursing again and would never hate anyone so fiercely.

Returning home and seeing it with fresh eyes, Kira realized that she did not want to stay there another minute. Why live in a place where every little thing reminded her of the past?

Kira quickly put the house up for sale and took her things to her mother's. She even gave the house a facelift for potential owners. Kim had paid for all the procedures but became more reluctant to give her money once she was in remission. Kira had to return to work as soon as possible. If she was being honest with herself, the thought terrified her. She had been broken for too long. She was afraid to go to interviews, afraid to communicate with clients, and afraid to talk about herself.

Another year flew by. Kira worked at a publishing house, finding advertising contracts for the magazine. She did not like the job since she was capable of a lot more, but she had no choice. The pay was decent and enough to live on. Considering that Kim's child support payments covered Olivia's needs, Kira even set some money aside. She got used to her new life without a husband, and no longer noticed that she continued to converse with him in her head. Kira had no intention of getting married again, although she went on dates. She did not really like anyone and could not understand the reason. Perhaps it was her past experience or perhaps the loss of trust in the opposite sex.

Something clicked when she received a message from an older and once handsome man. Kira was recovering after breast reconstruction surgery and had absolutely nothing to do. The ensuing communication brightened up her days in hospital, and the days thereafter. The man's name was Massimo, he was 10 years older than Kira and lived in London. Perhaps this was why Kira started corresponding with him, thinking that they would never meet. Six months later, Massimo decided to visit Kira, which upset her. She had no desire to meet him, convinced that she would lose interest once she saw him in person.

When day X came, Kira put on her best dress, which accentuated her slender figure, did her hair, and went out to meet the man waiting for her at the entrance to her apartment complex. Massimo was much more attractive in real life than in his photos. He was a tall, fit man with a shock of silver hair. The grey suited him. Kira was flattered that he was picking her up in a good car and had even brought a bouquet of flowers. She could not remember the last time she had gotten flowers.

Both were awkward at first, but after half an hour, the

embarrassment disappeared, and they spoke as warmly as they had over the phone. While saying goodbye to Massimo at the door, Kira somehow ended up inviting him in.

The next morning, Massimo prepared breakfast while Kira lazed about in bed. He turned out to be a good man. A former firefighter, he now owned a small bookstore. He was well-groomed, caring, witty, placid and incredibly good-natured. Kira was not giddy with happiness, and there were no butterflies in her stomach, but for the first time in many years, she suddenly felt at peace. Taking a deep breath, she stood up when she smelled the bacon and eggs.

"I've taken charge in here," Massimo smiled at Kira.

"That's fine," she replied. "I'm flattered."

"What time do you need to leave for work?"

"I'm already late," Kira laughed.

"Let's have breakfast and I can give you a lift if you like. I also have a surprise for you tonight."

"I'll make my own way there, thanks. And I doubt we can do anything in the evening. Olivia will be back from her dad's."

"I see," her date sighed. "Okay, no surprises then. We'll just have tea."

So began her long-term romance. Massimo would fly over to see her whenever he could, but she started visiting him too, where she met his children. They were older than Olivia, but still lived with their father. They were quite friendly and showed no jealousy towards their father's new girlfriend. Kira reminded them of their late mother in some way.

Massimo's house was small but cosy. Some rooms were empty. It had clearly been lacking a woman's touch for some time. The house was a little unkempt, which Kira tried to ignore.

They celebrated New Year together. Olivia liked London, as well as the family of her mother's boyfriend. She quickly befriended Massimo's children and spent most of the trip outside, visiting the various parks and attractions.

Massimo was restless when the time came for Kira to return home. His heart was heavy, and he did not want to let her go.

"I've been thinking," Massimo announced suddenly, closing Kira's suitcase, "but I couldn't bring myself to say it. I kept putting it off."

"Has something happened?" Kira tensed, seeing how agitated her partner was.

"No, no, everything's fine. Kira, I... I never thought my life could go from drab to something so bright and incredible! I never thought I'd meet a woman who made my heart soar. I love you and I want us to be together. Will you be my wife?" With these words, he took a box with a lovely ring out of the pocket of his pants and waited for Kira's answer.

Kira had clearly not expected this. She was flattered by the gesture, but not even in her wildest dreams had she imagined marrying Massimo. Her analytical mind immediately began to consider which continent they would live on and where one of them would find work. What about his children if he was the one who moved? His eldest daughter was studying at a prestigious university. Could Massimo leave her here alone, taking the younger children with him?

All this time, Massimo remained kneeling, and his face

reflected the full range of emotions. "I moved too quickly, didn't I?" he wailed.

"No, of course not!" Kira snapped out of her reverie. "I was just wondering how we would make it work."

"So, you agree?"

"Yes."

Massimo slipped the ring on Kira's finger and whispered, hugging her tightly, "We'll make it work! I promise."

On her return home, Kira considered how to organise her life from now on. There was nothing keeping Kira in this city, except her mother. She decided to discuss the situation with her.

"Of course you should move!" Mum snapped. "You're still a young woman so you'll be able to follow your usual model: husband, wife, a life together. There's nothing binding you to Kim anymore. Olivia will head off to university. You shouldn't stay here just for my sake!"

"I don't know," Kira still had doubts, although deep down, she knew the real reason for postponing the decision.

The same evening, she dialled Kim's number with shaking hands.

"Is Olivia okay?" he asked without preamble.

"She's fine. First of all, hello."

"Hello."

"I want to tell you that we're going to London."

"But you just came back from there!" Kim was surprised.

"You don't understand. I'm moving there for good."

Kim was silent.

"I'm getting married," Kira announced solemnly. Her soul rejoiced, and a spiteful smile appeared on her face.

"Married? To whom?"

"His name is Massimo and he's a bookstore owner."

"I see. Well, congratulations. What about Olivia's school? Have you decided where she'll go? Or will she stay here with us?"

This was not how Kira had imagined this conversation unfolding. "Sorry, Massimo's on the other line. I'll call you back," she replied and hung up.

Throwing the phone on the bed, she pressed her cold fingers to her face and burst into tears. "You're such an idiot," she scolded herself. Deep down, she thought that if Kim found out about the upcoming wedding, he would exclaim, rush to declare his love for her and beg her to stay. But he was living a completely different life, one that did not include Kira. All this time, Kira could not accept that the past was in the past and there was no way back. Not that she wanted to go back, she simply wished that none of this had happened. But it had already taken place a long time ago. A pity that she could not accept this fact, despite all the trials she had gone through.

Thus began a new chapter in her life called "New life, new country, new me". She liked London, although it took her some time to get used to the mindset and habits of its residents. But she refused to fall in a heap and focused on assimilating no matter what the cost. Plus, she was not there alone but with her family.

She quickly cleaned up Massimo's house and rearranged it to make it more comfortable. But living with another person's offspring turned out to be quite difficult. Kira could see that the years spent without a mother had not had a good effect on the children. Massimo had done his best to make their life easier after her death and had not noticed that he had spoiled them rotten. Kira would clean the house, but it would turn into a rubbish tip soon after. They expressed no thanks for the dinners she lovingly prepared for them. Nor did they respect Kira herself. She was a stranger to them. Dad's girlfriend was one thing – here one day and gone tomorrow – but a wife was quite another. Kira could not fail to notice this. In addition, Olivia's teenage behaviour threw Kira off balance. Her daughter constantly and mostly without reason complained about her new stepbrothers and sisters, refusing to show her mother any understanding. Kira wondered if she had done a good job raising her daughter.

Things were not going well with work, either. No one would hire her. Massimo offered her a job as the store manager, but Kira did not want to work under the same roof as her husband again.

She struggled to get used to her life in London. The city itself was fascinating with its centuries of history and the important figures who had once walked these streets, but for Kira, it was not home. Not that there was anything to tempt her back to her hometown. The only thing that kept her warm in this foggy world was Massimo's love. He loved Kira with heart and soul and tried to do everything he could for her. Their honeymoon never ended and Kira, who had not experienced such behaviour before, even wondered if this ever happened in real life. Her husband could not take a step without touching his wife and admiring her beauty, even when she was not her best. He helped in the kitchen and washed the dishes. As she considered her current marriage, Kira finally realized that her first attempt had not been a partnership, but God-knows-what. What had kept them together? Their work, their business, Olivia? Of course, their love had seemed eternal and irrevocable back in their student years. Looking back now, Kira understood that it had been youthful infatuation that never grew into true, strong love. Real love was not about rainbows and unicorns, it was, first and foremost, the desire to make life easier for the other person. It was about friendship, respect and so on. Kira had made Kim's life as easy as possible, but what did she get in return? Kira understood a lot. She no longer regretted what had happened. Her heart was at peace, but not for long.

One day, when she came home from the store, she found her daughter in tears. Olivia's face was red, and she looked just like her baby photos.

"What happened?" Kira asked, dropping the shopping bags.

"Mum," Olivia whined, "they're bullying me!"

"Who is?"

"These new relatives," Olivia replied, her fingers indicating air quotes. "Bianca came home from uni and was gossiping about me with Mikki. They were really loud just so I'd hear them."

Kira sighed heavily and grew tense. She would take her daughter's side in any situation. "What exactly did they say?"

"They called me princess. They talk about me with contempt. *"Oh, here comes Miss America"* and so on."

"Right. I'll talk to them."

"What's the point? I want to go home. I'm sick of living here and I miss Dad!"

"What do you suggest?"

"Let's go back?" Olivia said hopefully.

"Honey, it's been less than a year since we moved. You liked it here."

"And now I don't!" Her daughter said stubbornly. "I want to see Dad and Grandma."

"You can go to Dad's for the holidays."

"No. It's not the same. Let's go home."

"Olivia, you'll head off to university in a year, and what about me? Will I remain alone at home, constantly hearing about "Dad has this and Dad has that"? How he's got a wonderful life with his new wife and their cute kid?"

"Don't listen then! No one is forcing you!"

"But you constantly tell me stories without ever considering how much it might hurt or upset me."

"That's not the issue right now."

"I'll talk to Bianca and Mikki. I know it's hard for you, but we'll try to resolve this issue peacefully. Deal?"

"No deal. Whatever, I've got things to do." Olivia grabbed her phone and Kira realized that she was going to complain to her father.

So be it. Now Kim would know the sordid details of what was going on in their family.

The same evening, Kira told Massimo about what had happened, and he held a family meeting.

"I'm sure you've guessed why I've gathered you here," he thundered.

Olivia looked victorious. She was clearly enjoying what was happening.

"Today, and not only today, you said some rude things about Olivia. I don't like it at all! We're a family, and a family doesn't make fun of each other! Certainly not ours. Mikki, I want you to apologise to Olivia and promise that this won't happen again!"

"Dad, we were just joking!" Bianca smiled. "Olivia overreacted."

"Do I look like I find this funny?" her father went on. "I want everyone here to treat each other with respect."

"For that matter, we didn't start it. Olivia herself says far from nice things about us!"

"When was this?"

"She laughs about us with her father every day!"

Massimo looked first at Olivia and then at Kira. So, the way Kira presented the situation to him was not entirely true. He was annoyed that Kira had accused his children of being nasty.

"Well then, let's all agree that from now on, no one says anything unpleasant about the others. Isn't it much better to live in peace?"

The conversation was over, and the children went to their rooms. Massimo went into the kitchen, while Kira remained rooted to the spot, her face crimson with embarrassment. As she went up to Olivia's room, anger boiled inside her.

"Mummy," Olivia began cunningly, "it wasn't how they said it was. I wasn't really gossiping; I was just sharing things."

"Do you have any idea what you've done?" Kira asked, struggling to get the words out.

"I won't do it again. That's it!"

Kira could see that Olivia was lying. She most certainly would. Would she ruin Kira's chance of staying here?

She could not sleep that night, wondering what Olivia's life would have been like if she had stayed with her father.

Kim did not want her, he did not wish to waste his energy on raising her, and his second wife even less so. Olivia would have fallen in with a bad crowd, which would be followed by drugs, sleeping around, crime and God knows what else. Kira knew that she would never abandon Olivia and would raise her properly. It was her duty. Apparently, Olivia knew this too, which is why she was manipulating her mother.

The conflicts did not end there, and Kira suspected that Olivia was the cause of them. Her relationship with Massimo worsened, although he remained as friendly as before. Deep down, he found Olivia hard to tolerate and Kira understood this. She knew how difficult it was to love someone else's adult child.

The holidays were approaching, and Kira decided to visit her mother, whom she had not seen in a long time. Massimo remained back in London so that Kira could focus all her attention on her mother.

Nothing had changed at home, although after Massimo's house, her own seemed bigger and better. Olivia spent time with her friends, while Kira did not leave her mother's side, sharing her joys and sorrows. The holiday flew by, and it was time to go back.

"I'm not going anywhere!" Olivia told her mother when the tickets were already bought.

"Don't be ridiculous!" Kira could not believe it.

"I'm not kidding. I'm not going back there. You can go by yourself, but I'll stay with Grandma. You can come and visit us."

"Olivia! What is this? One, Grandma is old, so she won't be able to look after you. Two, you have school over there!"

"I want to go back to my old school. Veronica said that everything is the same, and they'd be happy if I came back."

"What about me? And Massimo?"

"Mummy, you only think about yourself! Who'll think about me? I refuse to return to that house! I'm not going and that's final."

Kira understood that she could not drag her daughter back by force and called Massimo. Perhaps, deep down, she did not want to go back either. In truth, Massimo's children got on her nerves too. It was not an easy conversation.

"I love you," Kira was saying, "with all my heart! But I can't put her in a suitcase and force her back to London, can I?"

"So, what are you suggesting?" Her husband asked resentfully.

"Olivia hasn't got long to go before university. She wants to live on campus with a friend. We'll visit each other until she graduates from school, and then I'll come back as soon as she gets into university."

Massimo considered his wife's proposal in silence.

"Be honest, you didn't come up with this today, did you?"

"I just thought of it now. Why do you say that?"

"It just feels like you used the trip to see your mother as an excuse, decided that you're better off at home and now, you don't want to come back!"

"That's not true, Massimo."

"Listen," he interrupted, "I know it's hard for you with my children, but can't we try to work through it? I don't want to lose you and live apart again."

"It won't be for long. Trust me. I don't want to be away from you either. But what else can I do? Olivia's my daughter."

"I understand…" Her husband said bitterly.

Massimo did not believe her words and knew that Kira was never coming back. Meanwhile, she would not admit this to herself.

Kira went back to working for the magazine and was welcomed with open arms. After being idle for so long, it was wonderful to be in the thick of things and surrounded by people. Kira felt needed, valuable and useful. Of course, she missed Massimo, but she was content. She went back to see her husband a couple of times, but something had changed in her. He saw it and she saw it too. Massimo felt like a stranger, and the life in London no longer felt like hers. They divorced quietly, without empty and unnecessary words.

Olivia went to university and Kira was left all alone, just like she had once predicted. Was she hurt? Of course! But she had to deal with this feeling somehow. She knew that children grew up and had to live their own lives but facing it in person was very tough.

One day, Kim called Kira. She had not heard from him in years. Kira was busy and had no wish to talk to him. But she figured that he would not have called just like that, so she picked up the phone.

"Do you remember how we met?" He asked out of the blue.

Kira frowned.

"Do you remember?" Kim insisted.

"I do. Why are you asking me this?"

"No reason. I just remembered the first time I saw you."

"Kim," Kira cut him off, "is something wrong? I'm not in the mood for sentiments right now!"

"Forgive me, Kira!" Kim suddenly began to cry.

Kira realized that he was drunk.

"I forgave you a long time ago. Calm down and tell me what happened." Kira asked, setting aside what she was doing.

"That snake cleaned me out. She took everything! Even the house."

Kira was silent for a moment.

"Didn't your mum arrange a prenup?"

"That's not the point. I signed the paperwork without looking, I was used to trusting her."

'Naturally,' Kira thought, 'she isn't like your foolish wife, who did everything for you once upon a time!'

"So? Is there nothing that can be done?"

"What can I do? I hired lawyers, but the signatures on the documents are mine, and I was of sound mind when I signed them. I don't know what to do! What should I do?"

"I don't know, Kim. You have my sympathies. I hope you find a solution." Kira ended the conversation and then stood in a daze for a long time.

'What was that?' She thought. 'Karma in action or the cycle of betrayal and hatred in nature? How do I protect myself from them? Avoid sinning? I don't think I've sinned, yet this has happened to me... Should I not trust people? But I can't live like this. What if I hadn't turned Kim into a businessman? What if he hadn't been wealthy? Would Asia have stolen him from this family anyway? The answer was obvious. It no longer mattered that he was also old, poor and sick. It did not make her feel any better. The best years of her life were gone forever.

3

Whose Fault Is It?

Whose Fault Is It?
A Story

"What a wonderful girl!" her father exclaimed when he first held the baby in his arms.

She really was a wonderful girl, but this would become clear later. In the meantime, she was a baby like any other – tightly shut eyes in a wrinkled and slightly puffy face. Yet he thought he had never seen anyone more beautiful in his life. His firstborn, his daughter! Just like he wanted.

Her parents decided to name the girl Antonella in honour of her late great-grandmother or Tonya for short. They worshipped her and loved everything about her: her sparkling blue eyes, her pale hair, and her stubborn, indomitable character.

Despite the early marriage and quick pregnancy, Tonya's

father Victor took his parental duty very seriously. He had not graduated from university due to falling head over heels in love, but he found a job, and not just one. He worked as an electrician during the day and unloaded trains at night. He did everything to ensure that his girls had maybe not everything but enough.

In the future, this driven young man would achieve everything he had dreamed of. He would build a small but successful business. He would build it brick by brick, until his very own car dealership stood in the city centre. Everyone knew him and he knew everyone, and his customers came from all over town.

Victor and his wife Lina did not change at all over the subsequent 20 years, perhaps becoming a little better and more impressive. Theirs was a loving family. Lina believed that she had been very lucky. Her life was exactly how she had wanted it to be. She had no regrets, although she occasionally wondered if she should have found a job back then.

Tonya was a good daughter to her parents. She did not misbehave at home, although her mother knew her better than her father. Tonya had great respect for Viktor and always tried to show him her best side. Her relationship with her mother was more like with a friend than a parent. Tonya could argue with her, even raise her voice sometimes or make fun of her. Lina did not mind this as she was still a child at heart. She had never truly grown up with such a caring husband.

Victor took care of all the challenges in life, hiding them from his girls. He was always giving them money for the best outfits and fancy restaurants. The family was living it up.

They stayed at a different resort every summer and came to see it as a given rather than a blessing. Could one say that they had become spoiled? Definitely! They did not live well, but very well, especially when compared to other people.

At the age of 21, Tonya was still living with her parents. She was satisfied with her life and had no desire to leave home. In the morning, she got into her German-made car and drove to university. She met her friends for lunch at popular places and was home by four. She spent her evenings with an unremarkable guy from a poor family and very bad company. It was strange that such a good girl had gotten involved with such a boy. He clearly did not deserve this gift. Tonya lavished money on him, not only buying him clothes, but also paying for his food. She was in no hurry to introduce the boy to her father because she was embarrassed. She did not really see a future with him anyway. Tonya did not want anything to change, such as getting married, and especially having children.

Tonya always spent her weekends with her dad. He took her to the lake or with him as he ran errands. She loved this time! She particularly enjoyed watching her father. She admired how he held one hand to his lips, how he gripped the steering wheel, and the funny way he squinted in the sun. Victor was a very handsome, athletic and well-groomed man. All of Tonya's girlfriends were in love with him and never missed a chance to flirt a little. Victor found it funny because he still loved Lina like mad.

The family planned a huge New Year's celebration that year. Tonya and Lina oversaw organizing and hosting this party. For some reason, they had decided that the theme would be black and white. Tonya believed that this colour scheme would make the event photos look especially luxurious. She went to the beauty salon on December 28th and asked the nail artist to make her nails look like a black veil. They turned out beautifully. If only she had known that the manicure would come in handy for a funeral rather than a party.

In the evening of the following day, Victor stopped by the store to pick up the last party supplies and saw an unpleasant scene that deeply troubled him. A young guy was beating up his girlfriend in the car park. Victor loaded his purchases into the boot and decided to stand up for the poor girl.

"Hey," he yelled. "Get away from her! Right now!"

The guy stopped and looked at Victor appraisingly. "Mind your own business, man!"

"I said, step away from her if you don't want to any trouble."

Victor slowly approached the couple. He was sure of his abilities and felt no fear that something might happen. No one could beat him in hand-to-hand combat. The young man tensed when he sensed Victor's strength and took a step back, releasing the girl. Victor was about to turn around and head back to his car when the guy launched himself forward and knocked Victor to the ground. Victor felt intense pain and a roaring sound that reverberated through his body. His vision went dark, and he thought that he had gone blind for a minute. The guy and girl jumped back in their car in alarm and drove away. Victor lay on the icy ground for a long time before he could get up. He was seeing double and felt very disorientated. He staggered to the car, found his phone and called Lina. When she arrived, she did not immediately understand that something terrible had happened to Victor. She drove him back home, chatting about inconsequential matters.

"So, you're saying that he pushed you?"

"Yeah."

"We should check the cameras to see who it was. Maybe the guys from the dealership can find him and teach him a lesson."

Victor groaned.

"What's wrong? Have you been drinking?" Lina asked worriedly.

Victor said something in reply, but she could not make out the words. Lina put her husband to bed and went to unload her purchases, coming back to check on him only an hour later. When she entered the bedroom, she noticed that Victor had not moved. Lina came closer and flinched when she turned on the bedside lamp. Her husband's eyes were bloodshot, and his body was cold.

"Tonya!" she screamed in horror. "Call 911!"

The ambulance arrived quickly. It was discovered in hospital that Victor had a fracture at the base of his skull and had been bleeding into his brain all this time. The doctors fought for his life, but it was too late. He died at 1 a.m.

Tonya could not believe that her beloved father was gone. She stared at her black nails and thought that they were at fault for what had happened. She banged her head against the wall and ran from room to room, convinced that Dad was alive, and this was all a terrible mistake. Worst of all, she really believed this. Even when his body was brought home and placed in the living room, she could not accept the truth.

"I know you're alive. Open your eyes. Please, Daddy, please!"

The sight of the distraught girl was heart-breaking for everyone present. In the commotion, neither Tonya nor Lina noticed how many people had gathered at their house. Victor's brother and business partner prowled through their bedroom for some reason, asking for certain seals and documents. Unfortunately, Lina did not pay this any attention at the time. Could you blame her? She was a woman still in the prime of her life, who had lost her love.

Life had to go on somehow after the funeral. A month after the tragic events, police found the guy who had killed Victor. A trial was scheduled, but it made no difference to Lina and Tonya, for it could not bring back their loved one.

Until the reading of the will, the women lived on the savings kept at home, with no idea that they were now practically beggars. It turned out that the car dealership, which Victor had owned with his brother, now belonged to his brother alone, and Lina and Tonya had no rights to it. Victor's bank accounts had also been cleared out. Lina had to summon all her willpower and go talk to Ray. When she entered her late husband's office, she was shocked by how different everything looked. The beautiful, lacquered oak table with Victor's initials was gone, and so were the family photos and the plants he had cared for. The office was now Ray's domain.

"Come in, my dear!" Ray was smiling.

"I wanted to talk to you about the inheritance."

"Oh, yes. What exactly are you wondering about?" He asked as if nothing had happened.

"Victor's half should have gone to Tonya, as well as the

bank accounts. He always said so. How is it that we've ended up with nothing?"

"Listen, Lina, you know how we built this business, right?"

"Victor built it, not you," the widow retorted.

"That's not important. I'm listed as the co-owner. I don't want a fight right now. Let's not spoil the family relationship."

"You've already spoiled it! All of Victor's heard-earned savings are gone. We have nothing! It's all yours now."

"Lina, it took many years to build this business and I doubt that you'll be able to run it properly. I don't want it all to go to waste. I'll hand over a portion of the profits every month."

"Hand over?" Lina could not believe the conversation she was having with a man she had always considered her family, whose wounds she had always healed.

"Well, yes. I don't see anything wrong with that. You might have to cut back on your spending, but your standard of living should remain the same. Besides, Tonya has almost finished university. It's time for her to find a job instead of hanging on to her parents' coattails."

"It's not for you to say when it's time for our daughter to do something!" Lina stood up abruptly, yanking her fur coat off the gaudy, ornate armchair.

"Where are you going? There's no need to get angry."

"The office looks like shit, just like its new owner." She spat on the carpet and left, slamming the door behind her.

A blast of frosty air hit her face as she stepped outside. Lina wanted to drop dead on the spot. She was so angry that she forgot to call a taxi and wandered aimlessly. For a moment, she forgot about her grief over Victor, hating him for leaving her all alone in this huge, cold world.

It was growing dark by the time she reached home. Tonya was shocked by her mother's blue and lifeless face.

"Mum, what happened?" the girl asked, rushing towards her.

Lina did not reply and went straight to the bar, reaching for a bottle of gin. Taking a sip straight from the bottle, she collapsed onto the sofa. "He's taken everything."

"How?"

"Just like that. He thinks that he had a hand in Dad's success, even though Dad hired him after the business was already well-established. Remember him back then? He had nothing! Nothing but problems, a divorce, and creditors at his heels. Victor had felt sorry for him." Lina burst into tears, burying her nose in the fur.

Tonya clung to her mother and stroked her hair, tears in her eyes. "Maybe we should hire a lawyer?"

"Don't you think he's already arranged everything in his best interests? It's too late."

The next six months passed as if in a dream. Lina and Tonya did not live, they survived. Every day was filled with pain. They could not let Victor go and would reminisce about what he had been like every night. They felt like his spirit had never left the house. His things still hung in the closet, and Lina wrapped her arms around them every time, inhaling the bare remains of her husband's scent. She still could not believe that he was gone, her heart still bound to him.

The money Ray gave them was far from enough. After a life of luxury, they experienced want for the first time. Lina was forced to sell most of her jewellery. It was humiliating, but the sense of hopelessness was even worse. She hated taking money from Ray, but she had no choice. Lina even tried to get a job, but no one would hire her due to a lack of experience.

The only joy in their miserable life was on the day they received their benefits from Ray. They would go to their favourite restaurant and pretend that everything was back the way it was. They had simply gone out as usual, and Victor was waiting for them at home.

On one of those evenings, Tonya met Idrak. When Tonya and her mother were about to leave, the waiter did not bring them the bill, but pointed to a man at the back of the room who had paid it. Tonya was already tipsy after the wine and thanked him in a rather vulgar manner, gesturing incomprehensibly. Lina was lighting a cigarette as she waited for a taxi and did not notice the stranger approaching her.

"Hello, Lina!" The man greeted her.

"Do we know each other?"

"My name is Idrak, we met at the car dealership."

Lina studied the man carefully but could not place him.

"We also met at the ski resort. My wife, Natalie, helped you with a jammed zip on your suit."

"Oh, my God! I'm sorry, Idrak, I didn't recognize you straight away. Hello!" Lina's face lit up. "So, you paid the bill?"

"Take it as a compliment. I heard about Victor and I'm sorry."

"Yes, thank you."

"Where's your friend?"

"She's my daughter, actually. Tonya, come over here and say hello to Dad's friend."

Tonya approached the man reluctantly and looked him up and down after a greeting. There was nothing remarkable about him. Idrak was a short man in poor shape. His eyes seemed pale, perhaps because of the rich red colour of his hair. The only pleasing thing about him was his smell, for he smelled exactly like Dad.

"Let's go, the taxi is here," Tonya said to her mother.

"I could give you a lift. My car is close by."

"Thank you but we can get home by ourselves," Tonya snapped.

On the way home, Lina scolded her daughter for her rude behaviour, but Tonya just waved it off. She had become increasingly impatient and short-tempered lately. All the character flaws that Tonya had hidden from her father had come to the surface.

The next day, a brand new, shiny BMW drove up to their house. The driver was in no hurry to get out, so Tonya had to go outside to get the unwanted guest off their property. As soon as Tonya appeared, the car door opened, and Idrak got out. He took an enormous bouquet of red roses from the back seat and said with a charming smile, "You certainly made me wait!"

"Then you shouldn't have waited. Why have you come here?"

"To see you."

"With flowers? Are you trying to hit on me?"

"Well, yes. Why?"

"Aren't you a little old for me? You could be my father!"

Tonya spoke impudently, yet something in her drew Idrak. Perhaps the fire in her eyes or the fire of her youth.

"You're certainly feisty! Shall we go for lunch?"

"I have other plans."

"Then let's have dinner. Give me your phone number."

Tonya thought that she would not say no to a decent dinner at a restaurant and gave the man her number. Lina came downstairs as her daughter carried the bouquet into the house.

"Who is it from?"

"From Idrak."

"My God!" Lina was alarmed. "He's married!"

"So what?" Tonya replied unflappably.

"No, this won't do. You need to nip this in the bud. I know his wife and I don't want you getting tangled up in something like this."

"Come on, Mum! What's going to happen? It's not serious. I'll just have dinner with him. I haven't been to The Willow in a hundred years."

"What if someone sees you?"

"No one's going to see us, it's Monday."

In the evening, Tonya put on the best of her remaining clothes and went out to the driveway at 7:00 pm, where Idrak was waiting for her. Indeed, the restaurant was empty except for the waiters. It turned out that Idrak had bought out the entire restaurant for the evening. Tonya found it funny. She did not hold back at dinner and ordered all her favourite dishes.

"How can you fit it all in?" Idrak laughed.

"I don't know, I like to eat."

For some reason, Tonya had fun with him. His jokes were just like her dad's, which comforted her.

By the time he took her back home, Tonya no longer cared about his appearance or his age. She kissed him furiously. This was the beginning of her affair with a married man. She initially thought that she would simply use him for his money, but before she knew it, she had become attached to him. Lina was not pleased about her daughter's behaviour.

"Do you know that his son is only 2 years old? Tonya, you must stop this. They went through around 10 IVF cycles before they had a baby."

"What's that got to do with me?"

"He has a family! His eldest daughter is your age."

"So, he has a daughter too?"

"He raised her. She's Natalie's child from her first marriage, but he raised her as his own."

"Right. Mum, Natalie is getting old. As far as I know, she's older than him, and the relationship has gone stale. You might say I'm strengthening their marriage. I bet that he comes home feeling guilty, prostates himself before her and showers her with gifts. She'd probably thank me if she knew that it was all because of me!"

"What if you found out that your father was doing this?"

"Well, maybe he did? How would we know?"

"How dare you say that! He loved me."

"Mummy, please calm down, I'm just kidding. Don't worry, nothing will happen. I'll dump him once he buys me a new car. All right?"

The years went by, and the affair picked up pace until the whole city knew about it, including Idrak's family. His wife feigned ignorance and still greeted her husband with the same smile. Their little son was growing up, the spitting image of his father, and Natalie hoped that this would outweigh the mistress. Fat chance! Tonya was trying her hardest to rip Idrak away from his family. Not so much out of love, but out of a sense of possessiveness. Even though he fulfilled her every wish and got her back on her feet after her father's death, it still was not enough for her. Tonya wanted him all to herself. She believed that she could be safe and stable only with him.

They were really living it up. Idrak enjoyed it after his bland life with Natalie, although he was noticing more and more how this behaviour was negatively affecting his health. He also felt pangs of guilt, especially under his eldest daughter's reproachful gaze. But he was unable to break the vicious cycle. Most likely, he did not want to. He tried to break up with Tonya once by changing his phone number and lying low, but his resolve only lasted a week.

One day, Idrak was forced to have yet another unpleasant conversation when he came to pick Tonya up.

"I'm tired of spending the night in hotels! They look at me like I'm a prostitute. Why don't we rent a place?"

"Baby, we've talked about these many times. I can't move in with you just yet. My family needs me, Natalie can't cope without me, and Angelo is still a little boy. Let's wait."

"I'm tired of waiting! It'll either be my way or the highway! I'm not joking, this is your final warning. You have to decide!" With that, Tonya got out of the car and stopped answering his calls. She was trying to wear him down.

Idrak drank heavily for the month he spent away from

Tonya. Natalie understood what was happening, and hoped that her husband would get through it, accept the breakup and their lives would return to normal. As soon as he felt better mentally, Natalie took Idrak to a rehabilitation clinic. A week of treatment got him back on his feet. Idrak swore off alcohol for good. He had developed an alcohol dependence during his time with Tonya, which had already damaged his liver. The news scared him. Idrak decided to give up not only alcohol, but also Tonya. Natalie's dream had finally come true, and her husband remained in the family.

In the meantime, Tonya was busy seducing a new beau, but only so rumours of him would reach Idrak. The guy was young, handsome and well-off, guaranteed to anger the older man. Yet nothing happened, or so it seemed to Tonya. The news reached Idrak as she had planned. He shrugged it off at first, but at night he suffered from insomnia, imagining his baby being caressed by another man at this very minute. He was at his wits' end and eventually went to see the guy. Idrak had a certain authority in the city and the guy backed off as soon as he learned that Tonya belonged to another man. 'This fight has been won, but what's next?' He thought. 'Tonya is a beautiful girl and she'll have a new man by tomorrow.'

As soon as morning came, he dialled the number he knew by heart.

"Hello," Tonya replied affectionately.

"It's me."

"I know. Are you going to offer me something?"

"No," Idrak was taken aback.

"Then why are you calling me?"

"I wanted to hear your voice."

"Heard it?"

"Yes."

"Then goodbye."

Idrak stood and stared at the blank screen for a long time. That evening, he decided to speak to Natalie.

"I can't do this anymore. You have to understand me and try to forgive me. I didn't mean to hurt you, but unfortunately, it has turned out that way."

"So, you're leaving after all?"

"Yes."

"Can't you see that she just wants your money?"

"That's not true. I feel young when I'm with her. Do you understand?"

"What about me?"

"I'm sorry. I don't know what to say."

"Do you have any idea how despicable this is?!" Natalie said bitterly. "You were in love with me since high school and I left my husband for you. I've been with you through thick and thin. I loved you for you, and not for your success. I fell in love with you when you had nothing, and I believed in you. You promised before God to be with me in sickness and in health."

"I'll provide you with everything you need. Things will remain almost the same as before. I'll still be responsible for you."

"Do you think that's what I'm talking about? You were my friend, my family! What about all the things we went through before we had Angelo? You were the one who wanted this child! Do you have any idea what it was like for me? All those procedures and miscarriages? What did I have him for? For whom?"

"Natalie, forgive me. I'm sorry, I didn't think it would turn out like this."

"You didn't think? You didn't think?!" Natalie's voice rose and there were tears in her eyes. "You were thinking. You must have been tired of being happy, so you wanted something spicier. You bastard! What are you doing to me and the children? How can look my parents in the eye now? How am I supposed to put up with all these pitying looks? The whole city is laughing at me! I refuse to divorce you! I'll take everything! Let's see how much love she has for you when you're left penniless."

"You need to calm down."

"I won't calm down! Get out and don't come back here again! Mark my words, this woman will drive you into the grave."

Natalie's voice was still ringing in Idrak's head as he packed his things. His heart was breaking for her and the children, but he still put his interests above others. Did he think that by abandoning his family and leaving his home filled with grief and pain, he would find his own happiness? No joy can come from causing someone else grief. But what if?

They rented a beautiful apartment Tonya had found. It had a large bedroom, stylish renovations, and a large, enclosed balcony with a view of the park. It cost quite a bit, but Idrak did not mind, thinking that he had found new happiness and a fresh start in life. He believed that he could live several lives in one, with a new woman and a new lifestyle. Tonya was a hurricane and life with her was an endless holiday. She laughed a lot, ate and drank a lot, and loved passionately. This was exactly what Idrak needed, for he was tired of the peace that all people strive for.

Six months passed since Idrak had left his family. He saw his son from time to time, but his adopted daughter severed all contact, viewing her father's betrayal as a personal insult. Natalie invariably gave Idrak a peck on the cheek when she met him in public to keep up appearances. It looked as if their conditional divorce had gone pretty smoothly. If only Idrak knew how much Natalie was suffering. She cried at night, her heart ground into pieces, but had to pretend she was fine again in the morning. Natalie refused to let Angelo see her tears.

Meanwhile, Tonya was enjoying her life with Idrak. Once again, she dressed in the best boutiques, went to the best resorts and could afford the life many people could only dream of. Her next goal was marriage, but Idrak resisted. Natalie would not grant him a divorce, so Tonya was forced to wait for Natalie to grow tired of this game. Idrak could insist on a divorce, but he did not want to take his wife to court. For now.

"I'll give him a baby and then he'll have to marry me!" Tonya once told her mother.

"I don't know if you should be forcing him." Her mother said doubtfully.

"Of course, I should! You must fight for your happiness – it doesn't just fall into your lap!"

"Tonya, I'm sorry, but your methods are pretty aggressive. I love you, but what good can possibly come of this? I saw

Natalie at the mall, she was as pale as a ghost. She didn't even say hello to me. She glared at me like I was the enemy."

"Oh, you make it sound like she was your friend in the first place!"

"She wasn't, but we crossed paths at events."

"I'm your daughter, not her! You should be thinking about my happiness. If it weren't for Idrak, we would have sold this house already. You should be grateful things have turned out this way. Thanks to Idrak, our life is the same as when Dad was alive."

Lina had nothing to say to this. She understood the truth of Tonya's words, but she also understood how awful the situation was. Lina would never have destroyed another family and would have died if Victor had done that to her. Lina applied every situation to herself. She felt genuinely sorry for the woman who had given her husband not only herself, but her whole life.

It was a stormy Independence Day that year. Tonya and Idrak went to a friend's country estate and partied hard as always. Idrak had drunk more than usual that day and could barely stand on his feet by 5 p.m. Tonya managed to put him to bed and continued to enjoy herself. He woke up closer to 11 p.m. and, finding Tonya laughing beside some guy, quietly said, "My stomach hurts. Let's go home."

"We can ask Steve for some medicine. Steve," she yelled, "Stevie!"

"Tonya, please stop shouting, I really don't feel well. Let's go."

Tonya studied Idrak and agreed to go when she realised that he was in a bad way. At home, she gave him a tablet for his stomach, which he promptly threw up, together with everything he had drunk and eaten that day. An hour later, he got out of the bathroom and went to bed.

Tonya awoke to strange noises in the middle of the night. Without opening her eyes, she reached out to Idrak and whispered, "Are you all right, babe?"

Her hand came away wet, making Tonya think that Idrak had vomited again. "Yuck!" she exclaimed and jumped out of bed.

She crossed the bedroom and turned on the bathroom light, screaming when she saw her hand, which was not covered in vomit, as she had thought, but blood. Rushing back into the bedroom and turning on the light, she tried to shake Idrak awake. He was drowning in a pool of his own blood. Finding the phone, she frantically dialled 911.

It was only at the hospital that Tonya realised she was still wearing her very short pajama bottoms and revealing top. She also saw her reflection, blood smeared across her hair and half her face. Sitting down on the cold floor, Tonya rested her head on her knees and waited. Her heart beat so fast she thought it might jump out of her chest.

"Dirty whore!" Someone said, and Tonya raised her head. Idrak's daughter stood over her. "Get out of here!"

"Elsa! Move away from her." Natalie said sternly, appearing out of nowhere.

More and more people were gathering in the corridor. Tonya understood that they were all related to Idrak in some way, either his or Natalie's relatives. She could not bear to be in the same room with them, for they all stared at her with condemnation and disgust. A doctor came out to see them at 5:40 a.m.

"Mrs. Lauren?"

"That's me," Natalie replied.

"I'm sorry to tell you this, but we couldn't save him. He suffered extensive haemorrhaging caused by alcohol intake. He had liver problems."

"No!" Elsa screamed and rushed at Tonya. Luckily, her relatives held her back. "It's your fault, you bitch! You killed my father! You're a murderer, a murderer! You stole him from us!"

Tonya covered her face with her hands and backed away. She burst into tears once she had run out of the hospital. She could not believe Idrak was gone. It had happened as swiftly and unexpectedly as with her father. She was alone again. Tonya wandered down the street as the city glowed in the morning sunlight. Someone rushed past her on the way to work, eyeing her with suspicion.

"It's not my fault," she kept repeating, "it's not my fault... It's not my fault."

4

The Choice

The Choice
A Story

As usual, she bustled around the apartment in her hurry to get ready.

"Can you keep it down?" Her fiance grumbled. "I'm trying to work, you know."

"Sorry, I just can't find my pass."

"Did you forget it at your mother's again?"

"Yes, probably. Well, I'm off. I've got to visit her anyway. Good luck with your writing. See you tonight."

Sonya kissed him goodbye, hurried outside and headed for her mother's house. As she walked along the familiar path every morning, she prayed furiously. Her mother had been fighting cancer for the past four years, and Sonya had been fighting alongside her. They had been to countless hospitals and transferred countless litres of Sonya's blood.

Her mother was still young, only 58 years old. She had always been a strong woman, but had given up when the cancer struck, and held on only thanks to her daughter. Sonya was her beacon of light, and every time she came, her mother imagined the cancer shrinking back from her daughter's radiance.

"Good morning, Mummy! How was your night?"

"Good morning, sunshine. I didn't sleep again. My back is so sore, I can't take it anymore."

"Well, let's have breakfast and it'll feel better. I brought you some porridge. Where's Dad?"

"He's gone skiing."

"Oh, lovely, he's made us some tea."

"How are things at home? How is Alex? Lounging around again?"

"Why lounging around, Mummy? He just works from home."

"Sweetheart, what kind of job is it if he doesn't get paid?"

"He'll get paid once he finishes the book."

"You've been saying that for the past three years."

"Do you want butter on your porridge?" Sonya steered away from the unpleasant topic, aware that her mother spoke the harsh truth.

The clock was showing 7:15 am when she ran into work. As luck would have it, the chief doctor was standing at the reception desk.

"Late again, Miss Poe?" she asked forcefully, and only the creases at the corners of her eyes betrayed her true mood.

"I'm really sorry," Sonya smiled apologetically.

"It's fine," the doctor smiled back at her. "I get it. It was a quiet night. Room 214 is on the mend."

"Oh, I'm so glad to hear it!"

It was a busy day as usual. Running from one patient to another, IVs, injections, paperwork, and helping the new doctors. Sonya got very tired, but she did not want to change jobs. She loved it, although once upon a time, at the beginning of her journey, she regretted not becoming a doctor.

She invariably visited her mother after work to measure her temperature and blood pressure, check that she had taken her medications, prepare the next batch for tomorrow, and squeeze her fresh juice. Her mum was sick to death of these juices, but she obediently drank them as instructed.

Sonya would finally stagger home, aware that she would have to do it all again tomorrow.

"Again?" Instead of a "hello", she was met with a question at the door.

"And good evening to you too."

"Do you know what time it is?"

"I stayed back at Mum's."

"Stayed back! You say that every time! You never spend time with me anymore. It's not fair."

"Alex, you know that Mum is sick. When she gets well, I'll spend all my time with you. What's for dinner?"

"I think there's leftover soup."

"Why didn't you cook anything? You knew that I'd come home late and have no strength left to cook."

"I was working!"

"I see," she replied calmly.

Sonya was a very non-confrontational person. She had

grown up in a caring and loving home and was unaccustomed to overt consumerism and brazen selfishness. It was different in her family, where Dad always took care of both her and Mum.

Standing over a boiling pot late at night, she remembered how she had met Alex. Back then, she thought he was nothing less than a genius. He was eloquent, courteous and well-groomed, and she could not have imagined that this handsome man would one day become a millstone around her neck.

The morning began as usual. She noisily got ready; he grumbled. Sonya was almost out the door when he suddenly said, "I forgot to tell you that we've got guests coming tonight. I invited the right people to promote my manuscript."

"Alex! How could you invite them without asking me first? Can't you see that I'm run off my feet at the moment?"

"I need this meeting. Surely you know how difficult it is for a writer to get their break these days. You've got to have connections! They need to be fed, watered, and so on. Don't be late, okay? And don't worry, I'll sort dinner out myself."

She did not answer, quietly closing the front door behind her.

"Has something happened?" Mum asked when she saw Sonya's face.

"No, Mummy. What makes you think that?"

"You look pale."

"Don't worry, I'm fine. Here, I brought soup and cheese sandwiches. Did you drink the juice?"

"I did," Mum replied, going into the small kitchen.

As soon as Sonya arrived at work, she was summoned by the chief doctor.

"You asked to see me, Mrs. Cahall?"

"Come in, Sonya. I wanted to tell you myself. Your mother's test results have come back."

Sonya grew pale. The results must not be good, or the doctor would not be speaking in such a tone. "Is everything that bad?"

"I'm afraid so."

"No," Sonya could not believe it.

"In any case, there are still treatment options available, so you must not despair ahead of time."

"The results can't be wrong?"

The head doctor shook her head.

Stepping out of the office into the noisy corridor, Sonya wanted to slide down the wall and burst into tears. Only one thought ran through her mind—how would she tell her mother? She could not destroy her hopes once again. It had happened so many times over the years! And yet she seemed to be on the mend this time and looked as if the disease had never struck.

"What's wrong, Sonya?" Her friend Lydia asked.

"The cancer is back."

Lydia, seeing that her dear friend was about to have a meltdown, took Sonya by the elbow and led her to the staffroom. She set her down gently on the sofa, gave her water and sat beside her, stroking Sonya's hair. "Alas, crying won't help! You've got to pull yourself together."

"Did you see what she was like after the last round of chemo? I don't think she can take any more!"

"Listen, don't think about that right now. Maybe she should redo the tests?"

"I thought about that too, but Mrs. Cahall said there was no mistake."

"Our lives are full of mistakes," Lydia smiled. "You should check again."

"You think so?" Sonya asked with hope in her voice.

Lydia's words helped to calm Sonya down, but she was plagued by doubt and fear throughout the day. She imagined her mother's face and the consequences of treatment, which made Sonya's hands tremble.

She did not visit her mother that day, claiming that she had to stay back at work. Sonya knew that she could not hide the sadness in her face, and even if she could, her mother was bound to guess the reason.

As Sonya drew near to her apartment, she heard thumping music and voices trying to yell over the top of it. She sank down on the cold steps and hid her face in her hands. "My God," she whispered, "I don't even have anyone to turn to."

She stood up and was about to return to work when the apartment door swung open, and Alex appeared on the threshold.

"Ah, you're here!" He exclaimed. "We've all been waiting for you."

Alex reached for her, and Sonya felt abruptly nauseous from the sharp and unpleasant tang of alcohol wafting from him.

"What's going on with you?"

"Nothing," she replied coldly, pushing him away from her.

Entering their small apartment, she discovered it crowded

with people. Half-naked girls tracked dirt across her carpet with their boots, leaving filthy shoe prints, while their companions did not bother to find an ashtray and stubbed their cigarettes on the table.

Looking around the home she had so lovingly painted and furnished piece by piece, anger rose in her. She walked up to the sound system, turned off the music and said, "Get out."

There was laughter.

"Huh? What?" mumbled a half-drunk girl, rising from a chair.

"I said, get out. Right now! Or I'll show you exactly what I mean!" Her stony face showed that she was not joking.

"Baby, calm down," Alex whispered, running up to her. "I told you about the right people..."

"I pay for this apartment, which means I get to choose whom I want to see here and whom I don't! There'll be hell to pay if the apartment isn't empty in a minute."

The guests dispersed astonishingly quickly. Alex was the last to leave, slamming the door so hard that the walls shook. Sonya lay down on the sofa. She wanted to scream, but she suppressed the urge and took some deep breaths. Before she knew it, she had fallen asleep.

When she awoke, she was not sure at first whether it was morning or still night. The clock showed 4. She stared at the ceiling, gathering her strength to keep on fighting. Sonya knew that she would not let her mother go and do everything in her power to save her yet again.

Getting up from the sofa, Sonya began to tidy the home. She was still nauseated by the smell of cigarettes, alcohol and strong perfume in the apartment, so she opened the windows to let in the frosty fresh air. Life would get easier from today.

She popped in to see her mother before work as usual. Her face betrayed nothing, so her mother did not discover the truth. Before she left, Sonya said nonchalantly, "Mummy, you seem to be feeling better, so it'd be good to undergo a full examination."

"What for?" Her mum tensed up.

"Don't worry," Sonya said and hugged her. "We should make sure that everything is OK, that you're getting enough vitamins and so on."

"You really think so?" Her mother remained doubtful.

"I'm certain! I'll be with you the whole way."

As soon as Sonya arrived at work, she went to see the chief doctor.

"Mrs. Cahall, Mum is willing to undergo the necessary procedures. Can you help me arrange it all, please?"

"Of course, Sonya. I'll talk to the doctors. I suppose we don't have much time. She should come to the hospital tomorrow. We'll do some more tests and an ultrasound."

"Thank you. I'm so incredibly grateful to you."

The whole day, Sonya was completely focused on her work. She was full of determination, which meant she had the strength to do anything.

Lydia came up to her and took her aside after the shift, whispering, "You're very pale. Do you want to talk about it? I'm always here if you need me."

"Thanks, darling, but I'm fine. Am I pale? I gave blood this morning, so that's probably why."

"Another transfusion?"

"Of course," Sonya smiled sadly. "It's for Mum. Don't worry about me. Everything will be fine."

"Hey, I'm supposed to be calming *you* down!"

Sonya hesitated as she approached the house. She did not want to deal with Alex right now. Two possible options awaited her: either he was not there, and she would have a quiet evening, or he was home and would be pacing around and sulking. If it was the second option, she would have to face a long and humiliating tirade for what she did yesterday. Deep down, Sonya already agreed with him, so she felt guilty even without his speech. 'I could have kept my temper in check,' she thought, 'especially since he'd warned me about the guests. On the other hand, could he not have held this event somewhere else? Not in our tiny apartment, where I return, exhausted, at the end of the day. Yes, now is clearly not a good time for guests. But when is a good time?'

Glancing at the windows, she saw that the light was on and sighed heavily. She entered the apartment quietly. Alex was watching TV.

"Hi," she said. He did not reply. "I know you're angry at me. I shouldn't have done what I did, but you've got to understand me too."

"You humiliated me in front of everyone!" He hissed.

"I didn't mean to. I found out yesterday that Mum's cancer has come back, so I wasn't up to receiving guests."

He was silent.

"Well, you can keep sulking. Yes, I was wrong, but you're no better. You should have invited them to a cafe or someplace else."

"I don't have the money for a cafe! That's why I invited them to our place."

"Funny, but it's not my fault that you don't have any money. You can work a normal job and write a novel at the same time."

"That's not how works of literature are created! Like you'd understand! I need to be fully focused on the task at hand."

"Whatever you say. I'm sick of having this conversation for the hundredth time. If you think I can keep doing this for years, you're wrong!" Sonya stopped short of telling him that she could barely stand him. This was not the fight she had to focus on.

The next day, Sonya arrived at the hospital with her mother. Nothing painful happened. The ultrasound was good, and the tumour marker tests would be ready by evening. Her mum was shaking a little, but everything went smoothly.

"Well done for being so strong, Mummy," Sonya told her afterward.

"I didn't think I could. I felt so nervous because I thought it was all behind me."

"Just be patient a little longer. Everything's fine, but it'll be even better."

They had a nice time together after the hospital visit, and Sonya returned to work in the evening for a night shift. The results of her and her mum's blood tests came back in the late afternoon. She opened her mother's envelope with shaking hands and stared at each number.

"There's no cancer," she said aloud and burst into tears, collapsing on the hospital floor.

Once she had calmed down, she checked the results again. "So, which one am I supposed to believe now?"

She did not open her own envelope. It was not important. What was important was surviving until morning so Mrs. Cahall could find out which result was the right one.

The next day, the head doctor heard about Sonya's conundrum and called the laboratory to find out what happened. As it later turned out, the first test results were incorrect, and the cancer was truly gone. What a relief that Sonya had not upset her mother unnecessarily!

"Mummy," she almost shouted into the phone, "the tests came back clear! You're healthy!"

"I knew it. I could feel it. You saved me."

"Well, really," Sonya said in embarrassment, "don't say that. I won't come over tonight, all right? I really need to get some sleep."

She raced home. The happiness rose in her throat, threatening to choke her. She desperately wanted to share the news with Alex, but he was not home. 'Oh, well. He'll be happy to hear the news once he gets home. Should I bake something?'

It had been so long since she had felt this way! There was no fear in her today, and she finally felt at peace. Fear, panic and anxiety had been her constant companions for the past few years. She would startle every time the phone rang, expecting bad news. Life would be much easier now.

As the faint scent of vanilla wafted through the apartment, Sonya decided to unpack her bag. She finally remembered about her envelope. Opening it, she could not believe her eyes. Could it really be more happy news?

She froze when she heard the key turn in the lock.

"Are you home?" Alex asked as he entered. "What is it?"

He looked at the envelope Sonya was holding in her hands. "I'm pregnant," she replied in shock.

Alex raised his eyebrows. This was clearly not a joyful reaction. "What are we going to do?" he asked.

"What can we do?"

"Right. Listen," he began, sitting down next to her, "I don't think this is a good time. We don't have our own place. I'm busy with my manuscript. Let's wait three years or so, get ourselves sorted out and then we'll try again?"

Sonya studied his face carefully.

"Why are you looking at me like that?"

"But it's already happened," Sonya said, touching her stomach. "and it's a miracle."

"I see," he said sharply and stood up. "I need to think."

When he left, she remained sitting in the same position, the envelope still in her hands. The smell of burning brought her out of her stupor.

The cake did not work out, and it did not work out with Alex either. Sonya wondered how she had lived for so long with this man. Why had she turned a blind eye to the fact that he was using her? He had never loved her. He did not know what love was. Love was not chemistry, it was friendship, support, empathy, warmth and compassion.

Only now did she realize what she had to do and how to keep going.

The next day, there was a phone call for her at the reception desk. It was Alex. He had come to the hospital and wanted to see her. Throwing on her coat, she went out to talk to him.

"Sorry I didn't come home yesterday. You stunned me with

the news. I've thought about it, and you need to have an abortion."

"No," Sonya replied harshly.

"I'm not ready for a child. I'm busy with other things right now. I have a career ahead of me and all these diapers and things aren't for me."

"Alex, it's already happened. I'm not going to have an abortion."

"You leave me no choice. It's either me or the baby!"

Sonya stood at the empty intersection and watched his retreating back. Lifting her head to the sky, she felt the cold snowflakes melt as they landed on her hot face. "How easy was that?" she whispered.

5

Playing Pretend

Playing Pretend
A Story
Dear diary!
The last time I wrote this, I was 12 or so. I didn't think I'd be keeping a diary again at the age of almost 30. Well, let's begin.

This morning, I visited a psychologist for the first time, and I'm scribbling in here on his advice. My name is Ellen and I'm 29 years old. I've been married for 8 years, and I have a daughter. It's like I've been playing pretend all my life. I kept waiting for the spotlight to shine on me and my bright and exciting "real life" to finally begin. It seems that I was wrong, deeply wrong. I used to be a model and imagined becoming world-famous and gracing the covers of all the top magazines. It's only now that I've realized that this won't happen. Young models, unencumbered by marriage and children, are breathing down my neck. I often wonder where I went wrong. It all boils down to that unfortunate day when I said yes to a marriage proposal. I guess I'm skipping ahead, so I'll go back to the beginning. I hope this really helps me—I'd hate to have wasted time and money on the session.

I was born on a very cold winter day. My mother really wanted me, although I'd never met my father. I found out only a couple of years ago that he had another family and had been lying to my mother about not being married. Not that it matters anymore. I had and still have a wonderful mum, and I had a wonderful grandfather instead of a dad. I'm grateful that he was able to replace my dad and give me the love that I might have been missing.

I had a pretty good childhood, except that we were always struggling financially. Sometimes, even to buy food. Mum had a hard time. She worked from morning to night to give me what I needed, but as you can see, it isn't always possible in this complex world. I remember that I was always jealous of others because their life was completely different to mine. Even back then, I thought that I'd grow up and show them for all the teasing I'd experienced. Although, to be honest, no one really teased me. One girl out of the whole class doesn't really count.

Since Mum had me quite late, she was 100% ready for motherhood. I'm talking about love and sacrifice, not money, of course. I think she even indulged me too much. Nowadays, when I look at my friends, I think she should have been stricter with me. She should have made me study harder or something. Even though I graduated from music school and also attended art school, I never used any of it. So, I didn't really learn anything useful

My modelling career began at 15, when I finally persuaded my mother to send me to modelling classes. I remember that she was very reluctant, but eventually agreed. I attended these classes for about a year, and at 16, I received an offer to go to China. My mother was afraid to let me go given that I'd never left my small town, let alone crossed the ocean. The trip cost money: to buy some things, visas, tickets, I don't remember what exactly. My mother already had 3 loans, so she struggled to scrape this money together. She borrowed money from literally everyone.

The tickets had been bought, my things were packed, and my mother and I drove to the neighbouring city where I was supposed to catch my big flight. Nowadays, it might sound strange to be flying for the first time at 16, but that was my experience. Was I scared of being completely alone in a strange city and culture? Of course! In truth, I was still a child and had no idea that it could have been a different kind of job, rather than modelling. Thank God I was spared such a fate. I heard many stories later about how the modelling career of some girls flowed seamlessly into prostitution.

Finally, there I was. I met my agent and the driver. I was taken to quite a spacious apartment, full of girls from all over the world.

The climate in China didn't suit me, so I was constantly sick. Plus, the food didn't agree with me at all. I had frequent stomach aches and nausea. I remember standing for 12 hours in heels with a temperature of 39 °C. All I could think about was not fainting. Agents, photographers, and especially customers don't care about your well-being. They spend time and money on you, and you're nothing more than cheap furniture to them, so they want to get the most out of you. The work was hard and exhausting, but I tried warding off feelings of fatigue as much as I could. During particularly tough moments, I imagined returning home and my mother and I going to the bank to repay the loan. This motivated me and kept me going. Many girls went to the clubs after work, for which they were paid extra, but I refused. Firstly, I wasn't interested, and secondly, I was afraid of getting into trouble.

The three months dragged on yet seemed to be over in the blink of an eye. I had flown to China with a small suitcase that I'd borrowed from someone, but I returned home with three. I bought so many clothes! For myself, mum, grandfather, my cousin and my friends. I scrimped and saved every penny I'd been given for travel and dinners. That's how it was.

I was so glad to see my mother's face at the airport! Sometimes, it felt like I'd never see her again. I was like a little girl again, loved and cared for.

My dream of repaying the loans came true. My earnings covered two of the loans, making life much easier. But the money I earned disappeared quickly, which meant that I needed to work again. Once I'd gotten a taste of money, I could think of nothing else. I wanted it so badly. I wanted to buy myself and my family whatever my heart desired, instead of wearing someone else's hand-me-downs.

While I was in China, I mistakenly believed that I'd never return there, but I changed my mind once all my savings were gone. How long did I go for the second time? I can't remember for the life of me. I remember that the second trip felt much easier than the first. How many trips were there? I can't be bothered to count them. In the end, China enabled me to pay off my mother's loans, which she had taken out for me anyway; to undertake a snazzy renovation of our place and furnish it with expensive furniture, and most importantly, to gain self-confidence. I thought it would always be like this. Money gave me freedom, but it also awakened my worst qualities. I became arrogant, bossy, quick-tempered, and at times even cruel. I fancied myself the queen of the world and even took it out on my own mother, accusing her of achieving nothing in life except endless debts. Not like me! I'm ashamed to remember it now. I think I've been punished enough for that.

I took useless courses at university so that I could get a simple job. I didn't do it to work in the field, but so that I had a backup option. Of course, I didn't think I'd use it as the imaginary catwalks of Paris and Milan beckoned. But the degree was completed and safely put away on a shelf in a silver frame.

And I'm flying overseas once again. Over the years of modelling, I'd come across some pretty poor specimens, their lives full of drugs, alcohol and promiscuity. I stayed away from all that. I was forever scarred by the suicide of a girl who'd lived in the same apartment as me. We hadn't been close, she'd lived in the back room, and we'd hardly spoken to each other, but what she did to herself shocked me. What made her do it? What had happened?

My final tour ended in June. I was about 20. I planned to return home and stay for only a month, but some depressing circumstances forced me to do otherwise. Yes, I came back, but I couldn't leave again. My grandfather passed away, only a month short of his 80th birthday. I knew that he would die one day, but I didn't expect it to be so soon. He had struggled with various illnesses for the last couple of years but had still held on. Unfortunately, the last setback proved too much for him. Mum was inconsolable. She had now lost her father, and she felt like she'd only recently buried her mother. Mum felt lost and lonely. She was no longer someone's beloved daughter. I couldn't leave her alone, so we started living together again. I had changed during my years of travelling, as I'd already written, so living with me wasn't easy for my mother. I found many of her habits and manners annoying, and the worst thing was, she could see it. It wasn't only my mother who infuriated me, but the town I was forced to live in again. After the bright lights of Shanghai, my hometown seemed terribly dreary and dim. I caught up with old friends and listened to boring stories of their petty little lives, but my thoughts would be far away.

Social media was becoming more and more popular, and I took my chance. I started posting everything I could, hiding my location, of course, because my former colleagues were subscribed to me. Was it then that I became addicted to pretending to be someone I'm not? Or maybe I was successful, beautiful and confident? I can't remember anymore.

One day, I got a message from a guy. The photo showed an equally successful, handsome and confident young man. I studied his page and saw all the attributes of a life of luxury: cars, apartments, parties and vacations. Was that what motivated me to go on a date with him? I can't remember that either.

I liked Albert right away. He was a tall and muscular guy, 5 years older than me. On our first date, he gave me a bouquet of roses and took me to the most expensive restaurant in town. At the end of the evening, I understood that he was a serious guy with clear goals in life, who wants to build a family.

"Mum," I said then, "can you imagine guys his age saying such serious things? And he has a wonderful family! His dad owns a spare parts company. His mum and dad have been happily married for almost 30 years. Can you believe it?"

At the time, my mother was ecstatic that I'd snagged such a handsome young man. She would proudly show her friends photos of Albert and would always add, "Here's our CEO!"

She wanted me to settle down, have children and live an ordinary, simple life like hers.

Three months after we met, Albert proposed one snowy winter evening. It was unexpected and just like in the movies. I can't remember where I'd returned from, but when I entered, I saw flickering candles and scattered rose petals leading deeper into his huge apartment. When I reached the dining room, I found the table set with flowers, candles, glasses and a bottle of champagne on ice.

"Albert," I called, "are we celebrating something?"

He appeared silently and when I turned around, he was standing on one knee. "Will you marry me?" Albert whispered.

I said yes. This was how my life and I changed forever.

His parents took charge of organising the wedding. They

also paid for it. All I had to do was choose a dress and show up on the appointed day. I have to say, they did everything quickly and in the best possible way. Although I dislike looking at the photos these days, filled as they are with lies and deception, I must admit that they turned out beautifully. You could easily put these photos on the cover of a wedding magazine.

Yet his father gave me a hint about what was going on when he made a toast. "Well, Ellen," he said, "I wish you all the best! We can finally sleep in peace because Albert is your problem now!" He laughed so loudly that I can still hear the echo of it.

The second warning came not long after. When we got to the honeymoon suite, Albert changed. He no longer joked and clowned around and stopped pretending to be sweet and friendly. He rudely sent me to bed and sat down to count the money we'd received at the wedding. This was the last time I saw the "family budget".

I asked him about the money when I decided to make his bachelor pad more suitable for a couple.

"I want to buy some appliances, rugs, lamps and plants. Shall we go shopping?" I asked.

"We'll buy it, but not now. Money's tight at the moment." he replied.

"What about the money we got at the wedding?" I asked softly.

"It's all gone."

I was shocked. I had seen a wad of cash in his hands that night. "What happened to it?"

"I had to invest it in the business."

"But you work for your father. I thought he dealt with such matters."

"That's not strictly correct. It's not just the business. I had a couple of loans that had to be urgently repaid. There was a problem at the warehouse—some expensive parts went missing and to avoid upsetting my father, I had to borrow money to replace them."

"Why didn't you tell your father?" I was surprised. "It means there is a thief working for you. You need to find him and punish him."

"Of course. You don't need to get involved; I'll sort it out myself."

Sure you will. I was sad to realise that my family life was beginning with lies, debts and loans. But then I thought, who doesn't have loans? My inner voice disagreed. 'Surely not the family money?' But I replied, 'What else is there? We're a family now, which means we must share everything.' Plus, he was doing it to protect his father.

A month or so after the wedding, Albert began to pressure me to have children. He was busy cleansing his body and encouraged me to do the same. I didn't want children yet because I was only 21, but I gave in under pressure.

"It's a bit early, of course," My mum said, "but on the other hand, you don't have to build a career. You're married and everything's fine. You've worked hard in China so you can take it easy now."

I think I fell pregnant on the first try. Everyone was ecstatic when they heard the big news, but my joy quickly changed to constantly feeling unwell. I had terrible morning sickness. Everything I ate or drank came straight back up. I lost a lot of weight and was afraid to look at myself in the mirror. The only person who supported me was my mother. I got nothing from Albert. He was at work all day and didn't even come home some nights. He didn't spend weekends with me but went fishing with his friends. Why did I put up with it? I couldn't let go of the dream that we had a marriage, a family and all that. If I'd known then that he was a liar and a thief with debts across the city, perhaps things would have turned out differently!

Things only got worse after Gerda was born. Thankfully, my mother stayed by my side and was always there for me, even though she worked at a job that was quite tough for her age. Albert showed no interest in his daughter. I confronted him about his behaviour, still hoping to save our relationship. After all, divorce sounds terrifying when you think about it the first time. It's only much later that you realise that there's nothing terrible about it. In most cases, it leads to salvation.

I remember the first phone call I got from the bank. I was rocking Gerda to sleep and was very annoyed that the phone kept buzzing even though I repeatedly rejected the call. When I heard the harsh tone of the bank employee, I felt like I'd been doused with a bucket of ice water. He mentioned a loan so large that I couldn't wrap my head around it. We could easily live for a year or more on such an amount. I frantically dialled Albert's number and hissed into the phone, "Why the hell are you in debt again?"

"What are you talking about?" he began evasively.

"Don't you dare lie to me! I just had a call from the bank! You even wrote me in as a guarantor! Have you gone mad? I hate all these debts. I've been running from them all my life, and for what? To run into them again!"

He mumbled unintelligibly, something about his father again, but I was no longer listening.

"I'm going to call your father right now and tell him what happened!"

"Don't, he has a weak heart. I'll sort it all out, I promise."

"Do you understand that you made me a guarantor? So, I'm responsible for this loan too?!"

"No, no. You misunderstood. I only added you as a contact. You've got it all wrong."

What a fool I was. I believed him again. When it seemed like things couldn't get any worse, I discovered that absolutely anything could happen in life. Especially if you're living not with a friend, but with an enemy, a pest. I learned again what it felt like not to have food in the house. I was so ashamed in front of my mum and friends. I told everyone that I was fine while crying into my pillow every night. At the time, I couldn't comprehend that I needed to take life into my own hands. I wanted to remain small and for someone else to take care of me. Despite living in another country and earning money, I was still a child inside.

The lack of money and endless problems had a terrible effect on my health. I was breaking, unaware that the cause was Albert and not our troubles. He began to treat me so badly that I didn't know how to react, having never experienced such behaviour before. Now we have the term "abuser", but I had no concept of it back then. The insults and humiliations became commonplace, and I began blaming myself instead of realizing that he was at fault. I still haven't quite figured out how the mind of a person living with a tyrant works, but I'm trying very hard. Yes, he didn't hit me, but he hurt me emotionally.

When Gerda turned 2, I was able to send her to daycare. Even though it was a struggle for us, I had to find a job, because I didn't have two pennies to rub together. I couldn't afford to buy anything. My mother loaned me money for study, and I became a lash artist. The first clients started coming to my home. It wasn't much money, but it was better than nothing. Then I learned how to shape eyebrows, which provided a little additional income. I tried my hardest, but life didn't get any better. Back then, I wondered why God didn't reward my efforts and sent me these trials. I understand a little better today. Perhaps I wasn't the kind of person who deserved something good. Frankly, I was awful! I schemed and badmouthed people, not even stopping to consider if my words might ruin someone's life. I loved drama, rumour, gossip and emotional rollercoasters. I don't know where it all came from. Was it the modelling life, where every day was like a new episode in a melodrama?

Here I'm writing that Albert was the worst man and father, but I was no better. I turned out to be a terrible mother. Maybe I loved Gerda, but not with all my heart like I should have. Definitely not the way my mother loved me. I'm ashamed to say that I hit my daughter and began to take my anger out on her quite early on. Anything the little mite did wrong would set me off. Instead of simply explaining that it was wrong or dangerous, I would resort to physical force. Her white angelic face would grow blotched with tears, and the places I struck remained red for several days. I took out my anger on an innocent child who couldn't fight back. Isn't that what Albert was doing to me? Abuse begets abuse. Will you ever forgive me, my precious?

Oh dear, I'm getting carried away here, but what's written is written. I'll move on.

Although I worked hard, money was still tight, but at least I could finally afford a cup of coffee in a cafe. Sitting in a cosy place surrounded by busy people, I felt like a human being again, unlike the creature I turned into thanks to my husband's daily insults.

Little by little, I began to model for local magazines and newspapers, advertising various items. Next, I received an offer to become the face of a well-known clothing boutique in the city. I received a small salary and, coupled with my earnings, I felt freer. Yes, I still couldn't buy myself anything expensive, but I could finally spoil myself a little. The freer I felt, the worse the situation at home became. Albert didn't like that my photos were in newspapers and on billboards. He called me names and constantly checked my phone. These awful scenes took place in front of our child. Gerda became anxious and cried constantly, flinching at every loud sound.

On her third birthday, I decided to organize a grand party with children's entertainers, guests and a huge birthday cake. Albert paid for everything. I didn't know where he'd gotten the money, and I didn't want to know. The party was going great, but I was deeply offended by a conversation I had with his father. He came up to me while the kids were watching magic tricks.

"Ellen," he said, "I'd really like you to review your spending.

I know that you're a young family and have a child, but there's a limit to everything. Albert's constantly borrowing money for one thing or another. It's all to do with you."

I didn't know what to say. My face turned red.

"What money are you talking about?" I asked, my voice trembling. "He doesn't give me a cent. I have two jobs. He doesn't buy Gerda anything."

"Ellen, I know it's embarrassing to admit it when I've just confronted you about it, but please think about what I've said. Maybe don't buy yourself such expensive dresses, for example," he replied, touching the sleeve of my new yet old dress. I'd actually bought it at a second-hand store.

He walked away, but I stood rooted to the spot. My mood was ruined, and there were tears in my eyes. I couldn't believe Albert was taking money from his father and saying that it was for me. "Where does it all go?" I wondered. The party didn't end there. Another creditor approached me not long after. It was the wife of Max, Albert's best friend. She asked when we, Albert and Ellen, were going to return the 50,000 Albert had borrowed a year ago.

"This is the first time I'm hearing of this," I said, embarrassed.

"Right." Martha shook her head. "We've been hearing how he's going to repay the debt tomorrow for the past six months. He said it was for your clothing business or something."

"I don't have a business."

"Interesting. Well, it's your family, but Max still won't put pressure on Albert, and I just don't know what to do anymore. We want to renovate the house and we urgently need this money."

"He'll give it back in the very near future!" I blurted out.

This was the last straw. I struggled not to make a scene right there, in the middle of the event. I stared at Albert's happy face as he laughed with the guests and could not understand what kind of person he was. I confronted him as soon as the guests left and the room was empty. I refused to listen to his lies any longer and didn't mince words, cursing like a sailor.

This time, he told me the truth. It turned out that he had stolen the parts from his father's warehouse to cover one loan and then another. He would take out a loan, struggle to repay it, and take out an even bigger loan at another bank. As a result, he had about ten different loans, and the total amount was several times more than the price of our apartment.

"What are you going to do?" I asked, dumbfounded.

"I have three businesses besides my father's. I hope it all works out, and I'll repay everything."

"But why all the lies? You should have told your father the truth from the start and admitted to stealing the spare parts. Do you realize what a snowball your little lie has turned into?"

I didn't know what to do. Why didn't I leave back then? Because I felt sorry for him, instead of Gerda and me. He said that neither his father nor his mother had ever loved him, that he had lied because he was frightened of them, and that he had no one but Gerda and me. I believed him. I thought, poor Albert, no one understands him except me! I would save him; I would help him somehow.

Our relationship improved a little after he told me the truth, and the verbal abuse stopped for a while. I thought that we could fix this mess together. For some reason, I asked my mother to take out a loan to repay Albert's debt to Martha. It was yet another mistake. Albert took the money without a twinge of conscience, promising to give it back, but he never did. Foolish me.

Things got more interesting after that. I was tidying up when Albert ran into the apartment. He was on edge, and I understood only later that it was nothing more than a show for me.

"What's wrong?" I asked.

"My father is kicking us out of the apartment."

The rag dropped from my hands, and I turned to gaze into Albert's face. "How is that possible? What happened?"

"I didn't want to tell you, but he's been bad-mouthing you over the past few years. He's said some awful things. He was against the marriage and said that I should divorce you."

'Yet another undeserved stab in the back,' I thought. "And what have I done to displease your father?"

"I told you not to return to work! Your photos are plastered all over the city! He says that a decent woman shouldn't allow other men to stare at her!"

"It's my job!" I jumped to my own defence, unaware that his father had nothing to do with it. Albert's plan was to sell the apartment under a stupid pretext and pay off part of the debt. The people he now owed were not from the banking world and did not like to be trifled with. He told his father that his cruel words had killed our marriage and told me that story about his father. A classic game of playing the victim. So pathetic, too.

But let's return to the conversation, which quickly escalated into a fight. Albert called me names again, and really struck a nerve. In that moment, I regretted telling him so much about myself. Albert said unforgivable things about my mother, the father who had abandoned me, and the poverty I lived in. He claimed that my work in China did not involve modeling but something quite different.

I was hysterical as I packed my things. My face was swollen from crying, and my hands would not obey me. Despite my state, I loaded my things and Gerda into a taxi and appeared on my mother's doorstep after midnight. I really frightened my mum and I'm sorry for that too. My marriage had a terrible impact on her, so that she looked like an old woman.

The next day, my mother received a call from Albert's father. He spoke blatant lies about how I'd ruined his relationship with his son, about what a spendthrift I was and what I'd driven Albert to. My mum is quite timid and defended me rather weakly. I was in no state to answer him myself. I was broken and found myself at rock bottom. I gathered my strength for three days and once I had calmed down a little, I dialled my father-in-law's number.

"Hello, do you have a minute?" I asked.

"Be quick, I have a meeting in 5 minutes," he replied rudely.

"You should know that whatever your son told you is a complete lie. I never took any money from him, so I don't want my good name to be dragged through mud. As far as I know, you've been insisting on a divorce. I can assure you that it will take place as soon as possible. Lastly, about being a spendthrift. In all the years of marriage, I've lived on handouts from my mother, and lately, on my hard-earned cash. Albert not only owes money to the whole town, but also to my mother. He stole spare parts from your warehouse to repay loans he took out for God-knows-what, but certainly not for me or Gerda. I'm done. You can sort the rest out yourself. Goodbye!"

I felt better after saying everything I wanted to say. Well, nearly everything. It's probably right that I didn't reveal how nasty their son was towards me. Speaking of Albert, he didn't stop texting and calling me the whole time I was at my mum's. He would send up to 100 messages per day. The morning would start with sweet words about how much he loves me, how wrong he was, and how he can't live without me. Then came the messages that if I didn't answer, he would kill me and then kill himself. Towards evening, he would change his tune and turn into a psychopath, writing unspeakable things. I'd never heard anything like it in my life.

A week later, he showed up on my doorstep with his bags packed. I didn't want to let him in, but he insisted that he had nowhere else to go, that the apartment was for sale, and that he was no longer speaking to his father. I can't quite remember what stories he told me, but I let him in.

Even though I had the divorce paperwork ready, I hesitated to sign it. Something stopped me. Fear, I guess, and the unwillingness to take responsibility for my life, my mother's and my daughter's. Plus, I didn't want to be a divorced woman. 'What will friends and people say?' I thought, unaware that everyone, absolutely everyone, couldn't care less about my life. Yes, they'd gossip for a couple of days, but then they'd move on. Their talk wasn't worth putting my life on pause. Well, I know that now, but back then...

For the first few months at Mum's house, Albert was as

meek as a lamb. He came home on time, bought groceries, and took Gerda for walks on the weekend. Albert spoke very respectfully to my mother, and once again, I wondered how such two different characters could live inside one person. This sweet, kind and funny person, and the other one.

Once Albert realized that my mum wouldn't hurt a fly, he showed his true face again. Now my mother's house shook too. I don't know why I didn't kick him out. Why did I put up with him? Fear, again. He threatened to take Gerda away from me, and when I received the long-awaited offer to go to China again for three months, I declined. I thought, what if he does something to the child in my absence, just to spite me?

It's worth adding that Albert had not only taken away my self-respect, but also the closest person apart from Mum, a cousin named Dana. She was six years older than me, but we had always been very close. She always loved me, defended me, and took care of me. She is no longer in my life and it pains me greatly. I'm just glad that she seems to be doing well. Do you miss me? I can only hope so.

Well, Dana never liked Albert. As soon as she heard about our first quarrel and the words my husband was calling me, she lost it. She said that no self-respecting man would treat a woman like that, much less the mother of his child. Dana was an excellent psychologist and a good judge of people. She knew how to set and protect personal boundaries. She was a proud woman and wouldn't tolerate any disrespect towards herself. I lacked the strength to do the same. In our conversations, I kept using the old excuse that I didn't have a father, so I didn't know how a man should treat a woman. She would remind me that I had a loving grandfather instead of a father.

Yes, it was difficult to argue with her. All my pathetic excuses came up against her rock-solid arguments. I played on her patience for a long time. I think she stopped talking to me because she was tired of my complaints and of witnessing my inaction.

"If you don't like it, change it," she would say. "Yes, things be difficult at first, perhaps very difficult, but it'll get easier sooner or later. Remember, you're not alone. You have you mum, and you have me. I won't let him have Gerda. I know a great lawyer. Anyway, who would entrust him with a child, especially given his debts?!"

I nodded in agreement but continued to do nothing.

"You see," Dana continued, "you have a child, a girl, who is witnessing all this. When she's an adult, she'll meet a jerk just like her dad, and he'll treat her the same way. It's awful! You must break the vicious cycle before it's too late. One, your marriage is based on a lie. Two, his father insisted on the marriage because he thought that married life would change his son. What is this relationship built on? There's no respect or support. Sure, a man might have financial difficulties. It's not a reason to leave him, but that's not the case here! He's lying! Constantly! Aren't you tired of living like this? Not only is he making the family suffer, but the story with these loans raises a lot of questions. Who is going to pay them off? Aren't you worried that it'll be you? What are you thinking? You should file for divorce immediately."

I filed for divorce only after we had lived with my mother for two years. What forced my hand was that Albert found himself in a corner and suggested it himself. Only then did he finally tell me where all the money had gone. He was a gambler. That's where he disappeared at night and that's what the loans were for. I still can't get my head around it. How can you gamble away all your money, your apartment, your whole life? But I took the news calmly. I was used to our toxic relationship, the threats and the debts by then. Why didn't I change anything? I couldn't see a way out, and I guess I was frightened. I thought that it would be difficult to escape in a small town and that Albert would keep pursuing us. Although Dana insisted that this was nonsense and men like him slinked away as soon as you fought back. But again, I wasn't that strong.

Oh, yes, another consequence of my indecision were problems of a feminine nature. The doctor said that it was due to stress and a lack of intimacy with my husband. He hadn't touched me since I got pregnant and didn't notice me as a woman. I found it insulting at first and I demanded that he fulfill his marital duty, but then I forgot. I gave up.

Today I feel ashamed for so many things. I remember how, on our seventh wedding anniversary, Albert pushed me because of some minor mistake, cursing me with all his might. Yet on the evening of the same day, I posted a photo from the restaurant with us clinking glasses and the caption "Here's to seven years of marital bliss." My God, who was I trying to fool? The people on the other side of the screen or myself? No one could tell that behind the bright and colourful photos hid a completely different individual! Why did I do it? So that people would think that I was no worse than them? The opinions of others again. Why did I care so much about them? Was it because I felt empty inside?

After 8 painful years, I finally broke free of this oppressive relationship. It happened as quickly as it had started. Albert wasn't home when I decided to pack his things and was very surprised when he saw the suitcases on the doorstep. I was calm, maybe even detached.

"Are you kicking me out?" He was indignant. "You know that I have nowhere to go, right?" His voice grew louder. He must have thought that it was another one of my quirks and that he'd crush my will once again.

"Raise your voice in my house again, and I'll call the police! Do I make myself clear?"

Albert wasn't prepared for this. I'd never spoken to him like this before. I usually cried and tried to resolve things peacefully.

"Where am I supposed to go?" He protested more gently.

"Your parents are alive and well. You can stay with them instead of living with someone else's mum and throwing your weight around here."

"What are you doing? It's New Year's Eve!"

"Yes, new year, new me, and a new life without you. I'm done."

"But what about Gerda?"

I just laughed. "Gerda is nothing but a way for you to manipulate me. The court will determine when you can see her."

"Don't destroy our family, Ellen! Do you want Gerda to grow up fatherless like you?"

"I've heard it all before and it doesn't bother me anymore. Take your things and leave. And don't you dare set foot in this house again."

And that was that. It turned out to be much easier than I'd thought. I understood, and most importantly, accepted it all.

I still don't know who I am, and I have a long way to go to find myself in this life. What I know for certain is that I don't want to pretend anymore, I just want to be! I want to be the real me. To stop pretending that I'm a happy wife and perfect mother. To stop caring about the opinions of strangers. To stop acting like I'm someone I'm not. I'm a woman like many others, with my own flaws, problems and bumps in the road. I'm still young and I can achieve something. Me. Without relying on someone else. I've learned my lesson.

The first step is always the hardest. I won't compare myself to people I don't even know, I won't obsess over their lives. I'll look only at myself and try to become the best version of myself. I promise!

6

The World of Snakes

The World of Snakes
A Story

Clara poured herself another glass of martini. Traces of prolonged drinking were visible on the face of this once beautiful young woman. Her waist-length hair was held back in a messy ponytail.

"What an asshole," Clara slurred once again. "It's been less than two months since I left, and he already has another chick in my bed!"

"They're all like that!" Her hanger-on friend Trish agreed.

"I'll send him to prison! I'll show him what's what! I hate him!"

A little girl ran out of the next room and interrupted Clara's tirade. "Mum," she yelled. "I want a cuddle!"

"My God, May, how many times have I told you? Go to your babysitter!" Clara replied irritably. "Can't you see the adults are talking?"

The babysitter rushed out to grab the child and dragged her, writhing, back into the room.

"He wanted her," Clara nodded at the closed door. "I didn't. It's like I could sense what was coming."

"You don't say!" Trish agreed once again.

Clara woke up around 4 a.m. at the same table. The alcohol had left an unpleasant taste in her mouth. 'How embarrassing,' she thought, 'to fall asleep at the table like an alcoholic!'

A couple of months ago, she could not have imagined that she would leave her home and find herself all alone in another country, while her dear husband sought solace in another woman's arms. Of course, they had had some trouble over the past year, but it had never occurred to either of them that they would soon be separate units.

How quickly had the past ten years flown by! So many things had happened in that time. His family's harassment of Clara and how he had stood up for her. And the lack of money, he dealt with that too. And the endless blackmail from dishonest business partners. For ten years they had fought against it all together, but now? Now she was an almost divorced woman with two young children, who drove Clara nuts with their endless questions about Dad.

The incident that would eventually break up their marriage happened a couple of years ago. Clara's husband had visited one of the city boutiques and met a stylist who worked there. The young woman, who mostly dealt with older married men, noticed Peter at once. He was young, rich and handsome. His bright green eyes, framed by black eyelashes, could seduce anyone, but it was not the eyes that mattered in this case.

It all started with simple text messages about new arrivals, but the young woman kept increasing the frequency of the messages. She started sending funny cat pictures and such. Clara did not pay this any attention, because she trusted her husband. Mistakenly, as it turned out. One day, the young woman showed up at their house alongside the family's best friend.

"This is my girlfriend, Veta," Connor had said.

Clara had only thought that it was a strange choice for Connor, because she could tell that those two were ill-suited for each other. She imagined someone sweeter, calmer and more homely with Connor. A woman who tried to steal the limelight at every opportunity did not suit him at all.

This was Veta's ticket into Clara's home. They even became friends. Veta, it seems, had seen all sorts of people in the boutique and had learned certain tricks of human psychology. She plied these skills on Clara and her husband. She seemed so smart, so understanding, and always listened so attentively. But it is the quiet ones you have to look out for.

Their family had been plagued by endless problems over the past year. It all had to do with money, as usual. People were after Peter, and Clara lived in constant fear for the children and for herself. She received threats too. The lawyers worked day and night to bring this dirty business to court, but it was a slow process.

During this time, Veta began to pour poison into Clara's ear. Veta said that she could not live like this, that Clara needed to leave for a while and consider the children's safety first and foremost. Her words made sense, and Clara thought that her dear friend wanted what was best for her. She began to seriously think about leaving. It would not be for long, and they would return as soon as the danger had passed.

Peter had not been in touch for several days when Clara bought the plane tickets to a place Veta assured her was safe. Nor did he not come home. His assistants reassured Clara that Peter was dealing with the problem and would be home soon, but the more time passed, the more Clara began to doubt.

"You need to leave right now," Veta said, appearing unexpectedly at Clara's house.

"What happened?" Clara asked, startled.

"It's not good. He went to meet the people who want to take his company away, but the negotiations aren't going well."

"How do you know all this?"

"I can't tell you! I've got connections."

"How can I go and leave him all alone?"

"That's not what you should be thinking about right now! They can use you to blackmail him! You need to leave today!"

"But I haven't got anything packed."

"Take a couple of suitcases with you. You can come back once things have settled down. Do you have money for the time being?"

Clara mentally calculated how much money she had and where she could go. Not her parents. Why worry them?

"Yes, I've got money," Clara returned to the conversation. "In the bank account. How much should I bring with me? I doubt they'll let me through with a bag of cash."

"Get ready, you can withdraw them all now, and I'll send them to you little by little."

Clara was doubtful. She did not want to leave anyway, and especially with so many machinations.

"What are you standing around for?" Veta insisted. "There's no time!"

Clara could not remember how she ended up at the bank and did everything that Veta told her. After that, she even helped Clara pack her suitcases and then escorted Clara and the children to the airport.

When Peter returned, he was shocked to find the house empty. There was no pitter-patter of children's feet, their laughter or their screams. Clara was gone too. Objects were scattered everywhere, and the house looked like it had been robbed. Clara's phone was disconnected. Peter was fuming when he rang the security guard who was supposed to watch his family.

"Where's Clara?" He roared.

"They left."

"Where? Why? What's with the house?"

"Veta took her. They packed their things."

"Why didn't you go with them? What am I paying you for?"

Peter did not wait for a reply and called Veta. She said that she would answer all his questions but only in person, because it was a serious conversation.

She quickly showed up and began to spin her lies, slandering Clara for all she was worth. Peter could not believe that his dear Clara would turn out to be such a woman. It turned out that she had long planned to run away, tired of the endless problems, and that she wanted to live peacefully at last. She did not want all these millions if she had to pay for them with her nerves. When Clara learned that Peter had gone to deal with the gangsters, she took her things, her money and flew away.

"She said it would be better if you were killed. She can't do this anymore."

Peter sat on the couch with his face in his hands. He could not believe that Clara would say such things about him and their life together.

"I need to hear it from her!" He told Veta.

"She's changed her phone number. She'll get in touch in a week's time for the next money transfer."

"What money?"

"The money she withdrew from the account. She told me to transfer it to her every week. Plus, the money from the sale of her jewellery. And the wedding rings."

"She sold our wedding rings too?"

Veta nodded.

"What about the children?"

"She said that you wouldn't see them again. And that you can finally make up with your family now that she's gone."

Veta worked on Peter all week, just like she had on Clara. Peter did not believe Veta at first, but what she said sounded too plausible.

When it was time to get in touch, Clara called Veta. Peter answered the phone. "So, you ran away?"

"Thank God you're all right!"

"I'm not all right!" Peter shouted. "Why did you leave? Why did you take the children? How could you?"

"Firstly, don't you dare raise your voice at me! Secondly, you haven't been in touch for ages! What was I supposed to think? We could have been kidnapped and held for ransom!"

"Who told you that? I was in negotiations! You idiot!"

The conversation turned in the wrong direction and ended with mutual accusations. This was all to Veta's advantage. She continued to pit the spouses against each other, gradually clearing a path for herself. How greedy does one need to be to destroy other people's lives without the slightest scruple? To make other people's children suffer?

Peter was like putty in Veta's skilful hands. She turned Peter against his wife, devaluing the years he had spent with her. She told him about Clara's flings, and even provided evidence. Nor did Veta stop singing her own praises and Peter, like many men, became hooked. Before long, Veta found herself in the marriage bed, which still held the scent of Clara's perfume. The next morning, Veta notified Clara of her new status, blocked her everywhere, and began to plan her new life as a millionaire's "wife".

Yes, such things can happen. The most terrible, vile and unimaginable scenarios are taken from real life.

So began a new stage in Clara's life. She had to keep living, but how? The feeling of resentment was the worse. She hated Peter, hated his assistants who had refused to put her in touch with him, hated Veta, hated herself, sometimes even the children, for they were exact copies of their father. She wanted to take the children and go back but dismissed the idea as soon as she imagined being turned away at the door. She thought Peter did not need her anymore. And she did not need him, not after he had betrayed their love with this snake. She did not have the strength to fight. Drowning her sorrow in alcohol was also not a solution. The consequences of those nights of drinking were terrible! Sometimes, she could not remember what she had done and whose bed she woke up in. Was she a traitor too? No, none of this would have happened if Peter had not started first!

The divorce papers she received brought her back to her senses.

"Well, that was fast!" Clara was indignant as she read the contract.

She signed the papers at once but tore them up in the same evening. "You won't get him that easily!"

Clara did not have a plan as such. She was not yet sure how she would punish Peter, but she would definitely get her revenge. Clara summoned her mother for help. It was unfortunate, but she had to be dragged into the family quarrel.

"I'll call his former partners and tell them about his weak spots! He'll be left penniless!" Clara declared to her mother.

"And then what? How will that help anyone?"

"I'll get sole custody of the children!"

"Another stupid idea."

"It will hurt him!" Clara's mouth twisted. "You know how much he loves them."

"Does he call them?"

Clara shook her head.

"Oh, Clara, Clara. How many times have I told you: keep your female friends away from your house! No, taking his parental rights away is not an option. It's the anger talking in you right now, but you need to think ahead. The main questions are: how do you plan to support yourself, what kind of future do you see for yourself and your children, and most importantly, where will you build this future? Revenge is useless! How are things moneywise?"

"I've got enough for now. Peter sends some over for the kids. He sent them clothes too."

"Right. First, you need to sort yourself out. I barely recognized you when I saw you. One, get rid of all the junk food in the fridge. Two, start going for walks. Three, get your sleep back to normal. You'll come up with a clear plan of action once you're feeling healthy."

Clara did the right thing in calling her mother. Although her mum was always quick with a comeback, she did provide good advice. Clara did everything her mother told her to do, and even a little more. First, she removed Trish, who was no longer welcome in her home. Clara had noticed that her friend was a bad influence on her, and that she just wanted money from Clara.

Next, Clara cut down on everything she could in food, and started going for walks. Her sleep did improve, although she had nightmares every night.

Life also continued back at home. Veta, being very cunning, yet still a fool, made one mistake after another. She assumed that the more mud she threw at Clara, the more disgust Peter would feel towards her. In reality, Peter grew cross with Veta. He disliked hearing the endless stream of bile about his wife and the mother of his children from morning to night. Veta pushed harder. She said that Peter must take the children away from Clara since her constant drinking made her a threat to their safety. Peter refused to believe it for he knew how much Clara loved the children.

Months passed and Peter's heart began to thaw. He began to look for excuses for Clara's behaviour and, deep down, had already forgiven her. Without her and the children, the house was completely empty, as if abandoned. Yes, it was so clean it sparkled, but Peter missed the objects scattered around the place. He has not heard his children's voices in four months. He wanted to see their sweet, rosy-cheeked faces, and one day, when he was in the parking lot, he unblocked Clara's phone number and called her. Clara was calm when she answered the video call. Peter thought she looked fantastic. He wanted to ask how she was doing, but she did not talk to him and quickly passed the phone to the children. He talked to them for two whole hours. He listened to the gentle babble of the younger one and empathized with the stories of the older one.

"Daddy, when are you coming back from the business trip?" asked 5-year-old Miley.

"Did Mum say that I'm on a business trip?" Peter was surprised.

"Yes, she said that you're busy with work, but you'll come back soon. I want to go on the merry-go-round with you. But just the two of us, okay? We won't take May."

"It doesn't seem very nice to go without her..."

"But she'll whine all the time, and we won't be able to ride properly!" the girl pointed out.

"We'll figure something out," Peter replied.

He stood outside his house for a long time after the conversation, wondering why it had all happened in his life. These squabbles, the money, the departure of his wife and children. In that moment, he wanted nothing more than to bury his face in Clara's wheat-coloured hair and feel as calm as he only felt with her.

The calls became more frequent and began to tug not only

on Peter's heartstrings, but also on Clara's. She missed her husband. The anger faded into the background. She admitted to herself that Peter had been a good husband for her, even perfect in some ways, and that they were well suited to each other. He was also a wonderful father, and Clara believed that no man could love the children the way Peter loved them.

"I want to go home," Clara once told her mother.

"Well, then, let's go. Dad is waiting for us. I know you probably don't want to return to our backwater town, but on the other hand, it'll be all so familiar to you."

"You don't understand. I want to return to my home, to Peter."

"What about the new girl?"

"She'll move over!" Clara narrowed her eyes. "He's my husband and I won't give him up. That's that. I've become convinced that she's spinning him stories about me and the kids."

"That's pretty clear. But how will you go back? How are you going to do it?"

"I have a plan."

A few days later, Clara bought a plane ticket and called Peter. "I'm flying over, and I'll be there in three hours. We need to talk. Come to the Ritz Hotel."

Peter's heart began to pound, and his throat went dry. He was excited to see Clara but also terrified. He did not know how their meeting would go or what it would lead to. After the events of the last six months, he thought that he would never forgive her "betrayal" and the words she had called him, yet life sometimes turns you in a completely different direction.

They met in the hotel room. Clara was cool but dignified.

She looked amazing. Peter did not know what to do so he sat down on the sofa and grabbed a pillow as some kind of psychological defence.

"You look great," he said.

"I know, but let's get to the point. Thank you for coming. You and I need to decide where we go from here."

"I just wanted to say..."

"Don't interrupt me, please. Let me finish. I won't take up much of your time. I wanted to tell you from start to finish about the last six months of my life without you. How I've been living and what I've felt in the past year."

Clara told her husband everything without embellishment. That she had feared for their children's lives and that she had felt lonely in their marriage. That she would never have left if her fear had not been magnified a hundred times by the woman he was now living with.

"I've always loved you, from the very first time I met you! Even your family, which had caused me a lot of grief, could not destroy my love for you. You know that. Yes, I may have been wrong at times, yet I've always wanted the best for you. I keep remembering the times when it was us against the world and we had nothing, not even a pack of cigarettes sometimes. We shared a room with your friend while his mother lived next door, yet I was happier back then than I am now or when I could afford to buy the whole new collection at that cursed boutique." Clara gazed into the distance and tears welled up in her eyes.

The truth that Clara shared made Peter's brain analyse the current situation. He understood that Veta had been deceiving him and using him all this time. Even worse, she was probably in league with his partners, who were still trying to pocket his business. He abruptly remembered all their conversations and the crooked game became obvious. How awful that he, so "great and powerful", had fallen for this cheap trick and had even lost his family because of it. Furthermore, Peter had told Veta things he should not have.

"Why aren't you saying anything?" Clara's question brought him back to the present.

"I'm going to tell you something but promise me that you won't get mad."

"Why should I be mad at you? We're strangers to each other."

"No, Clara, we're still a family, but that's not the point. I think Veta planned all this. They had to remove you so they could get close to me and take what we have."

"I don't understand."

"As you were telling me the horror stories Veta fed you, I realized the ultimate goal. They needed you out of the way so you couldn't give me advice. They needed to weaken me, deprive me of my family. I signed some documents that allow my partners to take certain actions."

"Are you an idiot?" Clara exploded.

"I am," Peter agreed. "But this won't help the situation. I'm going to step away from the business."

"What? You can't. You put so much effort into it!"

"I can and I want to, I think. They'll never leave me alone otherwise! They'll run the business into the ground anyway. When I started it, I had a higher goal—to help people with a useful product, but it has turned into something else. These snakes will rip each other's throats out, but I'll be far away by then. I'll build something new, and there'll be no place for such people in my business, just like in my home."

Clara knew how hard it was for her husband to part with his life's work, but maybe this was the right decision? "And the money?"

"We have enough for a couple of years. Then we'll figure something out."

"We!" She snorted.

"Yes, we. Will you come back home?"

Clara studied her husband carefully. His eyes shone just as they did many years ago and were brimming with love and guilt.

"I don't know if I can come back again. After her!"

"I'll rent us a new house, and we'll burn this one down!" Peter smiled, and Clara smiled too.

Two weeks later, Clara and the children returned to Peter. He rented a small but very cosy house where everyone was happy. The house was full of creative clutter again, but Peter was only glad of it.

The break-up with Veta did not go well. She threatened and tried to blackmail him, but he no longer cared. He was tired of listening to her poison.

After 6-8 months, the bodies of Peter's enemies began to float by, one after another, like a Japanese proverb come to life. The partners could not get the money because they had mismanaged the budget, and the company was rapidly heading for bankruptcy.

Veta scampered from one wealthy man to another but was turned away every time. She had lost her charm after being kicked out of her former place in such a humiliating way. O maybe all that anger she had been suppressing finally burst out. Who knows? But Veta was clearly insulted that some "moth", as she called Clara, had replaced a bright star such as herself. She could not understand that the same moth had been responsible for the success of the man she had pursued.

7

Thinking Out Loud

Thinking Out Loud

When I can't sleep, I imagine that I'm wandering through my life and the mistakes I've made. When I go back, I always correct them. I don't go somewhere, I don't say something, I agree to something, or I refuse something. I wander through my past, correcting what torments me and thus changing my present. It's now completely different. I no longer write books, I don't help people with my words, I'm not who I am today. Does it help me?

The pain of past mistakes, losses and breakups has left its indelible mark on me. Perhaps this pain helps me be who I am today? Having experienced many negative aspects of life, I have learned to understand people. I recognize their pain through my pain, and I know how to act and what to say to someone who needs it right now. It might be nice to expunge the shameful deeds from my past, but, first, it is impossible, and second, I wouldn't want to change as a result! So, I need to learn to be grateful for the path I've travelled and learn to live with what I have. I often wonder why we don't heed the advice of the older generation. After all, we received all the warnings, but we didn't listen. We did it our way, and it didn't work out very well. A pity that in those times, we always think that we are smarter and better than them, and things will, of course, be different for us. Poor fools. What's worse, or perhaps even more stupid is that our children will face the same situation. There'll be nothing left to do but watch our careless children rush towards the same thing that we once experienced ourselves. That's life.

But what is life? There aren't that many scenarios in the world and our lives are all quite similar. We rise and fall, suffer setbacks and defeats, and sometimes bullying and slander. There is joy and happiness, betrayal and loss. It's not easy, is it? Yet life is beautiful on the whole! Apart from hardship, there is love, hugs, smiles, laughter, kindness, happiness, friends and kindred spirits. Plus, the world in which we live is unique! The grass, trees, mountains, sun, sky, oceans and seas. What a shame that some people taint our existence in this miracle. They taint not only the world itself, but also the lives and destinies of other people. How does you protect yourself from them? I don't know. One thing I know for sure is that we must continue our journey, no matter what. No matter what!

I may be hopelessly foolish and naive, yet I believe that a day will come when the world contains so much more good than evil. Now, in the age of the internet, I see millions of kind and compassionate people supporting each other across the globe. I see people who know how to love and how to show compassion. As I observe all this, my faith in a better future can't help but grow. I want to believe that our children will be happier than us. I want to believe that every individual will understand that the world begins with each of us. I want to believe that people will value life more and notice the beauty in it more often.

I will continue to believe in you, my dear readers! Hardships pass and bright days will come. Most importantly, don't give up, don't let the darkness of pessimism and negativity seep into your heart and mind. If you fall, be sure to get up! If your life is in pieces, build a new one! Believe that, sooner or later, everything will be fine. Just stay afloat and row towards sunny horizons!

www.ingramcontent.com/pod-product-compliance
Lightning Source LLC
LaVergne TN
LVHW012244070526
838201LV00090B/114